FALKIRK COMMUNITY TRUST

30124 02506287 0

CANCELLED

Falkirk
Community
Trust

HOMEBOUND

2 1 NOV 2013

1 0 MAR 2014

2 3 OCT 2014

2 3 OCT 2014

3 0 OCT 2014

2 7 NOV 2014

2 7 FEB 2015

3 0 MAR 2015

3 0 JUL 2015

2 1 MAR 2019

- 1 AUG 2019

- 3 APR 2020

Bo'ness
01506 778520

Bonnybridge
01324 503295

Denny
01324 504242

Falkirk
01324 503605

Grangemouth
01324 504690

Larbert
01324 503590

Meadowbank
01324 503870

Mobile
01324 506800

Slamannan
01324 851373

This book is due
for return on or
before the last date
indicated on the
label. Renewals
may be obtained
on application.

Falkirk Community Trust is a charity registered in Scotland, No: SC042403

KU-750-267

ALSO BY ROBERT B. PARKER
FROM CLIPPER LARGE PRINT

Hush Money
School Days
Stone Cold
Blue Screen

Appaloosa

Robert B. Parker

W F HOWES LTD

This large print edition published in 2010 by
W F Howes Ltd
Unit 4, Rearsby Business Park, Gaddesby Lane,
Rearsby, Leicester LE7 4YH

1 3 5 7 9 10 8 6 4 2

First published in the United Kingdom in 2009
by Corvus

Copyright © Robert B. Parker, 2005

The right of Robert B. Parker to be identified as
the author of this work has been asserted by him
in accordance with the Copyright, Designs and
Patents Act, 1988.

All rights reserved

A CIP catalogue record for this book is available
from the British Library

ISBN 978 1 40745 658 4

Typeset by Palimpsest Book Production Limited,
Falkirk, Stirlingshire
Printed and bound in Great Britain
by MPG Books Ltd, Bodmin, Cornwall

FSC
Mixed Sources
Product group from well-managed
forests, controlled sources and
recycled wood or fiber
SA-COC-1565
www.fsc.org
© 1996 Forest Stewardship Council

Again, and always, for Joan

PROLOGUE

The Boston House Saloon was the best in Appaloosa. It had a long, teak bar with a big, gilt-framed mirror behind it. At night, the room was lit by coal oil lamps on a chandelier that could be lowered and raised on a chain and pulley. It was late afternoon, and the place was empty except for the bartender and three off-shift copper miners drinking beer. The bartender was Willis McDonough. McDonough was a fat man who always wore white shirts fresh from the Chinaman. He moved easily and with great dignity up and down the bar. He was polishing glasses with a clean towel when the two men came into the saloon and ordered two glasses of whiskey.

One of the men, the shorter one, had a small face with a narrow mouth and prominent front teeth, which he tried to conceal with a big, sweeping moustache. He carried a gun cross draw in a cheap holster. He wasn't a miner, and he wasn't a cowboy. The other man was taller, with a thick body and long, black hair that looked oily. He too had a gun. It was stuck into his right-hand pants pocket, with its dark walnut butt showing.

1

Between them, they drank a bottle of whiskey. They spoke only to each other. They paid no attention to McDonough or the three miners. When the whiskey was gone, they turned to leave.

'That'll be three dollars,' McDonough said.

Both men turned and stared silently at McDonough for a moment. McDonough looked back at them and felt uncomfortable. They both had guns. Looking at them, he realized, as if they had told him, that they would shoot him if he persisted. He didn't wish to die for three dollars. He shrugged.

'On the house, gentlemen.'

Neither one showed any reaction. They turned and left the bar. McDonough's heart felt shaky in his chest.

They had just come from seeing a stereopticon show about Venice, Italy. Now they walked up Second Street, lit mostly by the moon and a little by the light that spilled out of the barrooms. She put her arm through his. She could feel how strong he was. It would be so exciting if they could ever go to Venice – or anyplace, really, as long as they were together. Coming toward them on the board sidewalk were three men. From the way they walked, she could tell they were drunk. She wanted to cross the street, but he said no. He didn't cross the street for anyone. They met by the livery stable. One of the men asked them where they were going. He was a tall man, she remembered, with narrow shoulders and a walleye. His beard was scraggly, as if he had trouble growing one.

'We're going home,' her husband said, 'if you'll kindly step out of the way.'

'Good-looking lady you got,' the walleyed man said.

'My wife,' her husband said, and she could hear the warning in his voice.

'She fuck as good as she looks?' the walleyed man said.

Her husband hit him very hard, and he staggered backward. One of his friends, a short, thick man with no hat, drew his gun and shot her husband in the chest. She screamed. Her husband collapsed in a heap. The tall man got his balance back and dragged her away from her husband and into the livery stable. The two other men followed. They forced her onto the floor and began to take off her clothes. She struggled as hard as she could. Then she was naked and one of them was on her. She felt as if she was surrounded by a vast, empty space in which her own screams echoed like those of someone else. Then she closed her eyes and set her jaw and waited.

Jack Bell had worked all the tough towns. He'd been a city marshal in cattle-trail towns and worked the wild mining towns like Tombstone and Silver City. He'd scouted for the army and rode shotgun for Wells Fargo. He'd once arrested John Wesley Hardin. When Clayton Johansson's wife described the men who shot her husband and raped her, Bell was pretty sure who did it. With two deputies, he

3

rode out to the Circle RB ranch to talk with Randall Bragg, who owned the ranch and for whom the suspects worked. They met in the open area of hard, trampled dirt between the ranch house and the barn. Most of his hands stood near Bragg. All of them were armed.

'Randall,' Bell said. 'I'm afraid I need to bring three of your boys back into town with me.'

Bragg was a spare man, wearing a black duster and a high-crowned black hat. He held a Winchester rifle. Bell could see that the hammer was back.

'Can't spare 'em, Jack,' he said.

His voice was deep, but it had a hard sound to it, as if it were forced out through his nose.

'It's serious legal business, Randall. I got to take them in.'

'No.'

Bell looked at Bragg and the cowboys ranged behind him. He looked over his shoulder at one of the deputies, and nodded at the walleyed man standing with his two friends near one end of the group.

'Cut those three out,' he said.

The deputy looked uncertain. Bell's hand rested gently on his gun's butt.

'Do what I tell you,' Bell said.

The deputy moved his horse forward and pitched suddenly off the horse as a shot was fired from the barn. Bell knew it was a Winchester; he'd heard enough of them. He turned his horse toward the shot and pulled his gun free, and a bullet hit him in the

4

face and knocked him backward out of the saddle. The second deputy sat, frozen, in his saddle. He looked at the deputy and Bell sprawled in the dirt. He glanced at the barn and then at Bragg. Bragg, still holding the Winchester, smiled.

'Time to see what you're made of,' he said to the deputy. 'Ain't it.'

The deputy pulled his horse sharply around and headed out at a gallop. No one in town knew where he went.

CHAPTER 1

It was a long time ago, now, and there were many gunfights to follow, but I remember as well, perhaps, as I remember anything, the first time I saw Virgil Cole shoot. Time slowed down for him. He fought with an odd stateliness. Always steady and never fast, but always faster than the man he was fighting.

Like my father, I'd been West Point, and I was good at soldiering. But soldiering didn't allow too much for expansion of the soul. So after five years in the Indian Wars, I turned in my commission and rode away to see how far I could expand it. To keep from starving to death while I was expanding it, I shot buffalo for the railroad, and rode beside the driver on Wells Fargo coaches with an eight-gauge shotgun, and scouted now and then for the Army. I sat lookout for a while in a gambling parlor in Durango. I did a short turn as a bouncer in a whorehouse in Canon City. I got in a fight in Tres Piedras, and killed the man and had to move on pretty quick. I tried to find a little gold in the mountains in Colorado and didn't, and came down out of the San Juan Mountains, looking for something else to do. Along the way, I read a lot of books and fucked a lot of women, all of whom I liked. Now, with thirty dollars' worth of gold in my pocket, on a dark bay gelding named Sugar that I'd won playing poker in Esmeralda, I came on into Trinidad in the midafternoon on a summer day with the sun warm on my back.

It wasn't much of a town then. Two streets north and south. Three streets crossing east and west. Twelve blocks in all. It was one of those towns that existed mostly for people passing through. Cowboys who brought cattle to the railhead from the East Colorado grasslands. Soldiers on the way to Fort Carson. Hide hunters, teamsters, and miners occasionally, coming down to resupply. A few people trying to farm. People like me, moving from place to place because they didn't know what else to do.

As I passed the Rattlesnake Saloon on my left, the swinging doors burst open and a big man in a buckskin shirt came through them faster, surely, than he would have wished, stumbled across the boardwalk, trying to catch his balance, and fell forward into the street. There was blood on one side of his face. Sugar shied a little, and I pulled him up. The man in the street had gotten himself onto all fours when the saloon doors opened more gently and a tall man came out wearing a black suit. The suit's coat was pushed back on the right side to expose a big, bone-handled Colt. I could see the badge pinned to his

8

white shirt. Very dignified and deliberate, he stepped off the boardwalk into the street and stopped maybe six feet from the man in the buckskin shirt, and waited. Behind him, five or six other men pushed out of the saloon and stood on the boardwalk. He didn't seem to see them, but I noticed that he had turned slightly, so that he could look at the man in the street and the men on the boardwalk.

The man in the street was on his feet now. He was a big man, fat but strong-looking, with a black beard and long hair. His buckskin shirt looked as if he'd worn it since the buck was killed. On his belt, he wore a bowie knife and a big Army Colt in a flap holster. He smelled like a man who skinned buffalo. Some of the street dust had caked onto the blood on the left side of his face. He faced the man in the black suit.

'Goddamn you, Cole,' he said. 'You got no business hitting me with that gun.'

'Time for you to come on with me, Bear,' Cole said. 'Until you cool down.'

His voice was surprisingly light and soft.

'I ain't going with anybody,' Bear said. 'I paid that whore three dollars for an hour, and she fucked me once and said she was through.'

'Bear,' Cole said, 'I would guess that you are only good for one an hour.'

'Don't you rag me, Cole. Next time I see that sow, I'm going to gut her.'

'No.'

9

Cole's voice didn't get less soft, but something came into it that made the 'no' crackle like summer lightning. Bear almost swayed for a moment. Then he steadied himself, and his eyes shifted to the other men on the boardwalk.

Somebody said, 'We're with you, Bear.'

Somebody else said, 'Don't let him run you.'

Bear turned his gaze back to Cole.

'I ain't coming with you,' Bear said.

Cole didn't move. Nobody spoke. The light wind that had followed me out of the mountains drifted along the street, kicking up tiny swirls of dust and hay and dried manure. The force of his motionless silence was hard to explain. But I could see it pushing at Bear. The men on the boardwalk began to spread out a little. They were all hide skinners, probably come into town with Bear. Been sleeping on the ground with him, cutting buffalo with him. Eating bad food and drinking lousy whiskey with him. They couldn't back away from him now. One of the men slid the hammer loop off his Colt. I took the eight-gauge from under my right leg. Cole saw me, I knew. Already, I could tell that he saw everything. If he thought I was with the skinners, the increase in odds didn't appear to bother him. I had no money on this one. But I didn't think Bear should gut a woman, whore or otherwise, and I didn't think one man should go against seven.

'Marshal,' I said. 'I'm backing you in this.'

I said it softly, but it was so still that it almost

10

echoed. Cole didn't stop looking at Bear, but he made a barely visible nod. Bear still watched Cole. The men on the boardwalk glanced at me when I spoke, and spread a little farther. I cocked both barrels on the eight-gauge and rested the butt against my right hip. Then I moved Sugar a little closer so that I was nearly beside Cole. Again, the silence arched over us, made more intense somehow by the sound of the easy wind.

Bear said, 'Fuck you, Marshal,' and went for his gun.

I brought the shotgun to my shoulder. Cole seemed in no hurry. Carefully, he drew the Colt, thumbed back the hammer, aimed at the middle of Bear's big body, and shot him in the center of the chest. He recocked the Colt as he turned a half-turn so that the big, bone-handled Colt was steady on Bear's supporters. Bear sagged and fell over, his gun half out of the holster.

Sugar didn't mind gunfire. Sudden movement scared him, but noise had no effect. He held rock-still where I had set him, so that both barrels of the shotgun were steady toward the men on the boardwalk.

'You men go about your business now,' Cole said.

Nobody did anything.

'I won't tell you again,' Cole said.

At the far right edge of the group, the right shoulder of the man who'd loosened his Colt made a kind of involuntary twitch and then froze. Everything teetered. Then the man turned and walked away, and the rest of the group followed him. Cole carefully let the hammer down on his Colt. He opened the cylinder, extracted the spent shell, put in a fresh one from his belt, closed the cylinder, and put the Colt carefully back in its holster. Then he looked up at me and nodded.

'Come see me in my office when you can,' he said.

Then he turned and walked away without a glance at the corpse. I stayed there for a time, watching as some people came out into the street and looked at Bear and stood around, and finally a man in a white coat came along with a wagon, and four of us helped him put Bear in the back, and he drove off. I tied Sugar to the rail, took the shotgun with me, and went on in and had a couple of whiskeys in the Rattlesnake, and a plate of beans and bacon. Some people stared at me, but no one said anything and, feeling warmer inside, I went on down to the jail and sat in the front room where Cole kept his office, and we talked. He asked me my name and I told him.

'Everett Hitch,' he said.

Like he was tasting it.

He asked me had I done much gun work, and said I had done some, but no law officering. And he asked me what I had done, and I told him.

'West Point,' Cole said – not impressed, just recording it, like he did, and filing it.

'You didn't like soldier boyin'?' he said.

I told Cole that I liked some of it. I liked the men, and sometimes, on mounted patrol, I liked

12

the space, and how far you could see, and the way it seemed like possibility was rolling out ahead of us. But most of the time, I said, it was sort of crampsome.

'Nothin' can cramp you,' Cole said, 'if you don't let it.'

And I told him I thought that was right, which was why I quit soldiering and rode off to see what possibilities there might be. He nodded at that. I don't know if it meant he understood, or if it meant he approved, or if he was registering again. And filing.

'You quick with a handgun?' Cole asked.

I said I could shoot, but what I was really good with was the eight-gauge. Cole smiled.

'If she could pick it up,' Cole said, 'my Aunt Liza could be good with an eight-gauge.'

I agreed that it was hard to miss with an eight-gauge.

'You ever hear of me?' Cole said.

I said I had. Cole took out a bottle of pretty good whiskey and two glasses, and poured us a drink. And we drank that drink and a couple more.

'I need somebody to back me up,' Cole said. 'You and the eight-gauge want the job?'

'Sure,' I said.

Which is how, fifteen years ago, I got to be a peace officer and Virgil Cole's deputy. Which was why I was with him now, still carrying the eight-gauge, walking the horses down a long, shale-scattered slope toward Appaloosa.

CHAPTER 2

'They're living off us like coyotes live off a buffalo carcass, you know?'

'Everything eats meat likes a dead buffalo,' Cole said.

We sat at a round table in the saloon at the Boston House Hotel in Appaloosa. Cole sat back, out of the light a little, his face shadowed.

'They buy supplies in Olson's store and don't pay for them. They take whatever women they feel like. They use horses from the livery and don't bring them back. They eat a meal, drink a bottle of whiskey, whatever, and leave without paying.'

The speaker was a white-haired man with bright blue eyes. His name was Abner Raines.

'You in charge?' Cole said,

'Three of us,' Raines said, 'Board of Aldermen.'

He nodded at the two men with him. 'I own this place. Olson runs the store and the livery stable. Earl here owns a couple of saloons.'

Phil Olson was much younger than Raines, and portly, with smooth, pink skin and blond hair. Earl May was bald and heavy-set and wore glasses.

'And we got no law officers,' Raines said. 'Marshal's

14

dead with one of the deputies. The other ones run off.'

'These people cattlemen?' I said. 'Don't seem like good cattle country.'

'It ain't,' Raines said. 'Most of the money in Appaloosa comes from the copper mine.'

'So what do they do?' I said.

'Bragg's got some water up around his place, but they ain't raising many cows. Mostly they steal them. And pretty much everything else.'

'How many hands,' Cole said.

'With Bragg? Fifteen, maybe twenty.'

'Gun hands?'

'They all carry guns,' May said.

'They any good with them?' Cole said. 'Anybody can carry them.'

'Good enough for us,' Raines said. 'We're all miners and shopkeepers.'

'And we're not,' Cole said.

'That's for certain sure,' Olson said. 'I heard after you and Hitch came in and sat on Gin Springs one summer, babies could play in the streets.'

'That's why we sent for you,' Raines said. 'We're ready to pay your price.'

Cole looked at me.

'You game?' he said.

I shrugged.

'It's what we do,' I said.

A smile like the flash of a spark spread across Cole's face.

'It is,' he said, 'ain't it.'

The smile went as fast as it had come, and Cole turned his somber, shadowy face to the three aldermen.

'Money's all right,' Cole said.

'Then you'll do it?'

'Sure.'

The dining room smelled of cooking and tobacco and the lamp oil that kept it bright. The room was nearly full of men. The sound of cutlery and men's voices sounded civilized and normal.

'What do we have to do?' May asked.

'Tell him, Hitch.'

'Who makes the laws in this town?' I said.

'The laws?' Raines said. 'I guess we do: me and Earl and, ah, Phil. There's a town meeting twice a year. But between times, we do it.'

'Cole and me'll do the gun work,' I said. 'But we're going to button the town up like a nun's corset. And we need you to make laws, so we can enforce them.'

'We got laws,' Raines said.

'You're gonna have more. We need a lot of laws to make it all legal.'

'Well, sure, I mean, you tell us what you need,' Raines said, 'and if it seems reasonable, we'll put them right in the bylaws.'

Cole said, 'No.'

'No what?' Raines said.

'No,' Cole said. 'You do what we say or we move on. You solve your problem some other way.'

'Christ,' May said. 'That would mean you was running the town.'

'It would,' Cole said.

'We can't have that,' May said.

Cole didn't say anything.

'I mean, you're asking us, so to speak,' Raines said, 'to turn the town over to you.'

Cole didn't say anything.

'Far as I can see,' I said, 'you're gonna turn it over anyway. Us or Bragg.'

'But what if you ask for laws that we think are wrong?' May said.

Cole was entirely still.

Then he said, 'We'll give you a list.'

'A list.'

'A list of rules,' Cole said. 'You agree, we have a deal. You don't, we ride on.'

They all thought about it. The door in the hotel lobby opened, and it stirred the air in the dining room. The lamp flames moved in the stir, making the shadows shift in the room. The door closed. The flames steadied. The shadows quieted.

'Sounds fair,' Raines said after a while, as if he couldn't think of anything else to say.

'We'll bring you the list in the morning,' Cole said.

'I'll be here,' Raines said.

CHAPTER 3

We'd had a list of rules printed up five towns ago, and in the morning, Cole took them down to the hotel and gave them to Raines in his office. The laws were Draconian. The paper had a lot of aforesaids and wherebys in it, but, if you prune the thing to its essence, what it said was that what Cole said was law. Raines frowned as he read it and moistened his lips. Then he read it again. He looked at Cole. Then he looked at the paper again. The door of Raines's office opened suddenly and a round-faced little waitress came in. Her face was flushed.

'Mr Raines,' she said.

Her voice sounded foreign. Swedish maybe. She seemed short of breath.

'Not now, Tilda,' Raines said.

'Trouble in the bar, Mr Raines.'

'Can't Willis handle it?'

'It's Mr Bragg's men.'

'Jesus God,' Raines said.

He looked at us.

'Space for your signature down there at the bottom,' Cole said. 'On the right.'

Raines looked at us and at the paper. Cole never moved.

'There's four of them,' Tilda said. 'They have guns.'

Raines's mouth trembled very slightly, and I thought he was going to say something. But instead, he clamped his jaw, took out a pen, and signed the sheet. Cole picked it up, looked at the signature, waved it a minute to dry the ink, then folded it and put it inside his shirt. With no change of expression, he nodded toward the door and I went out. The bar was to the right of the lobby. You could enter it from the lobby, but most people went in through the street entrance on the opposite side. It was the kind of thing I'd learned to notice without even thinking about it. *Always know where you are*, Cole used to say.

I went straight through the lobby to the street, and turned right and walked to the corner and went in through the swinging mahogany doors of the saloon. The late-afternoon sun, slanting through the doorway, made the smoky air look sort of blue. I let the doors swing shut behind me and moved to the left of the door while my eyes adjusted.

The center of the room had cleared, tables had been pushed aside, and most of the people in the saloon were standing against the walls. Four men, all wearing guns, were drinking whiskey at the bar. Behind the bar, the strapping, red-faced bartender stood stiffly, not looking at anything. There was a big, brass spittoon in the center of the cleared space, and two of the men at the bar were trying to piss in it from that distance. Neither was having much success. Cole came into the saloon through the lobby door, and watched for a moment.

'Button them up,' he said in his light, clear voice.

One of the men faltered in his stream and looked at Cole.

'Who the fuck are you?' he said.

'Virgil Cole.'

'Virgil Cole? No shit? Hey, Chalk,' he said to his partner in piss. 'Virgil Cole wants us to stop.'

Chalk turned toward Virgil, his equipment still fully exposed, like his partner's.

'Step a little closer, Virgil Cole,' he said. 'And I'll piss in your pocket.'

Chalk was a skinny guy with a hard little potbelly that pushed out over his gun belt. He had a meager, shabby beard, and it looked, from where I stood, like he needed to trim his fingernails. His pal was tall and thick and had long hair like Bill Hickok, except Hickok's was clean.

'I am the new city marshal,' Cole said. 'Put it away or lose it.'

'Hey, Bronc,' Chalk said. 'They got a new marshal.'

The other two men, who'd been leaning on the bar, straightened a little and moved slightly apart.

'Didn't they have another marshal, 'while ago?' Bronc said.

'They did.'

'Keep using them fuckers up, don't they?' Bronc said.

'Got no use for them anyway,' Chalk said.

Cole didn't seem to mind the small talk. He seemed entirely relaxed, almost friendly, as he stood just inside the doorway from the lobby.

'Put them ugly little contraptions away,' he said. 'I'm going to walk you down to the jail, and I don't want to scare the horses.'

No one stirred in the room. It was like one of those high-plains days in the summer, when it's hot and still and a storm is coming and you feel the tension of its coming long before it gets there. Both men buttoned up their pants. It's easier to be dangerous with your breeding equipment stowed.

'You ain't walking us nowhere, Virgil Cole,' Bronc said.

He was squat and muscular, wearing a little short-brimmed hat. His gun was butt-forward on the left side, almost in the middle. The walnut handle looked worn. Chalk stepped a little way from Bronc and loosened his shoulders. His Colt was in a low holster, tied to his thigh. It had a silvery finish with curlicue engravings. Chalk thought he was a fast-draw gunman.

'You pull on me, either one, and I'll kill you both,' Cole said.

At the other end of the room, behind Cole, a thin man with no beard and limp, black hair took out a short revolver and held it on the tabletop.

21

Chalk and Bronc stared at Cole. Then Chalk laughed.

'Bullshit,' he said and dropped his hand.

Thoughtfully, Cole shot him before his hand ever touched the gun's butt, and he was already beginning to fold as the man at the back table raised his gun. I shot him. Bronc had his gun just clear of the holster when Cole's second shot hit him in the face and he fell backward against the bar and slid to the ground next to Chalk. The noise of the gunfire still rang in my ears. Cole was looking slowly around the room. No one moved. The fourth man held his hands high in the air; his face was pale, so the web of broken veins showed clear.

'I ain't shootin',' he said. 'I ain't shootin'.'

I walked over and took his gun out of holster and handed it to the big, red-faced bartender.

'I warned them,' Cole said, and opened the cylinder on his Colt, replaced the two expended shells, closed the cylinder, and put the gun away. It was one of Cole's rules: Reload as soon as the shooting is over. I put a fresh bullet in my own piece and put it back in its holster. Cole walked to each of the three down men and felt for a pulse. None had one.

CHAPTER 4

Cole and I rode up north of town one morning to look at the wild horses in the hills, a little west of where Randall Bragg had his ranch. They were there for the same reason Bragg was, because of the water. We sat our animals on top of a low hill and watched the herd graze in the sun on the eastern flank of the next hill. Seven mares, two foals, and a gray leopard Appaloosa stallion that looked to be maybe sixteen hands. The stallion raised his head and stared at us. His nostrils were flared, trying to catch more scent. His tail was up. His skin twitched. He pranced a couple of steps toward us, putting himself between us and the mares. We didn't move. The stallion arched his neck a little.

'They hate the geldings,' I said.

'Stallions don't like much,' Cole said.

'They like mares,' I said.

The stallion went back to grazing, but always between us and the mares.

'Virgil,' I said. 'I'm not minding it, but why are we up here, looking at these horses?'

'I like wild horses,' Cole said.

'Well, that's nice, Virgil.'

Cole nodded. The horses moved across the hill-side, grazing, their tails flicking occasionally to brush away a fly, the stallion now and then raising his head, sniffing the wind, looking at us. There was no breeze. Occasionally, one of the mares would snort and toss her head, and the stallion would look at her rigidly for a moment, until she went back to grazing.

'Easy life,' Cole said. 'They get through here, there's another hill.'

'Stallion looks a little tense,' I said.

'He's watchful,' Cole said.

'Don't you suppose he gets worn down,' I said, 'all the time watchful? For wolves and coyotes and people and other stallions?'

'He's free,' Cole said. 'He's alive. He does what he wants. He goes where he wants. He's got what he wants. And all he got to do is fight for it.'

'Guess he's won all the fights,' I said.

In a cluster of rocks on top of one of the hills west of us and the horses, several coyotes sat silently, watching the herd with yellow eyes.

'Foals better not stray,' I said to Cole.

'The stud knows about them,' Cole said. 'See how he looks over there. Foals are all right long as they stay with the herd.'

The sun was quite high now. Maybe eleven in the morning. Our own horses stood silently, heads dropped, waiting.

'Virgil,' I said after a time, 'these are very nice

24

horses, but shouldn't somebody be upholding the law in Appaloosa?'

Cole nodded, but he didn't say anything. And he didn't move. To the east of us, a thin stream of dark smoke moved along the horizon. The stallion spotted it. He straightened, staring, his ears forward, his tail arched. Small in the distance, barely significant, more than a mile away, a locomotive appeared from behind the hill, trailing five cars. The stallion stared. I could see his skin twitch. The train moved along the plain, toward Appaloosa. Then the stallion wheeled toward the herd and nipped at one of the mares and the herd was in motion, the stallion behind them, herding them, the foals going flat out, all legs and angles but keeping up.

We watched as they disappeared west over the hill, away from the train. And Cole stared a long time after them before he turned his horse east toward Appaloosa.

CHAPTER 5

We had a jail, but when there was nobody in it, Cole liked to sit in the saloon and watch what was going on. He liked to nurse a glass of whiskey while he watched, and so did I. We'd sit together most of the time. But if there might be trouble, we sat on opposite sides of the room. It was Cole who decided. It was one of his rules. Today we were on opposite sides of the room. While we were sitting and nursing, inside on a hot, bright morning, Randall Bragg came to see us. He walked into the saloon with half a dozen men, and paused inside the door and looked around while he waited for his eyes to adjust. Then he nodded his men toward the bar, and walked over to where Cole was sitting. His spurs jangled loudly in the suddenly quiet saloon.

'My name's Randall Bragg,' he said.

'Virgil Cole.'

'I know who you are,' Bragg said. 'We need to talk.'

Cole nodded toward a chair. Along the bar, Bragg's men had spread out, watching Cole. Bragg sat down.

'I see the big fella across the room with a shotgun,' Bragg said.

'Eight-gauge,' Cole said.

'Good idea, spreading out like that.'

'It is,' Cole said.

Bragg gestured toward the bar, and one of Bragg's men brought him a bottle of whiskey and a glass. Bragg poured himself a shot and looked at it, like he was thinking about it. Then he drank the shot down and poured himself another one.

'You a drinking man?' he said to Cole.

'Not so much,' Cole said.

'And Mr Eight-gauge over there?'

'Everett,' Cole said. 'Everett Hitch.'

Without looking at me, Bragg said, 'You a drinking man, Everett?'

'Not so much,' I said.

'Hard to like a man that don't drink a little,' Bragg said.

His high, black hat was set square on his head. Even sitting, you could see that he was tall, and the hat made him look taller. He had on a starchy white shirt and black pants with a fine chalk stripe tucked into hand-tooled black boots. His spurs were silver. His gun belt was studded with silver conchos, and in his holster was a Colt with white pearl grips. Cole smiled.

'But not impossible,' Cole said.

'Well,' Bragg said, 'we'll see.'

He drank most of his second drink and wiped the

corners of his mouth with his thumb and forefinger, pinching his lower lip in the process.

'You shot three of my hands,' Bragg said.

He wasn't looking at Cole when he said it. He was carefully pouring more whiskey into his near-empty glass.

'Matter of fact,' Cole said, 'I only shot two. Hitch shot the other one.'

I smiled and shrugged.

'Point is,' Bragg said, 'I can't keep having my hands come in here and you boys shooting them.'

'I can see how you'd feel that way,' Cole said.

'So we need to make an arrangement,' Bragg said.

'We do.'

Bragg smiled slightly and nodded. Everyone was looking at Cole and Bragg. While they were looking, I picked my shotgun up off the floor under my table and held it in my lap just below the tabletop.

'You have a suggestion, Marshal?'

'There's a set of town bylaws posted right outside the door of this here very saloon,' Cole said. 'Your boys do like the bylaws say, and everything will be *muy bueno*.'

Bragg's face pinched a little.

'And if they don't?' he said.

'Then I arrest them.'

'And if they don't go along?'

'I shoot them.'

Cole smiled sort of happily at Bragg. He nodded toward me.

'Or Everett does.'

I had moved the shotgun onto the tabletop. As Bragg looked over at me, I cocked it.

'That's your idea of an arrangement?' Bragg said after a moment.

'The law is all the arrangement there is,' Cole said.

'Your law,' Bragg said.

'Same thing,' Cole said.

The men along the bar were looking at Bragg and looking at the shotgun. Bragg sat silently for a moment, looking at Cole. Deep in thought, maybe.

Then he said, 'This town belongs to me. I was here first.'

'Can't file no claim on a town, Bragg.'

'I was here first.'

Cole didn't say anything. He sat perfectly still with his hands relaxed on the top of the table.

Leaning forward toward him, Bragg said, 'I got near thirty hands, Cole.'

'So far,' Cole said.

'You proposin' to kill us all?'

'That'd be up to you boys,' Cole said.

'Maybe you ain't good enough,' Bragg said.

I could see it in the way he sat, in the way he held his head and hands. He was trying to decide. Could he beat Cole? Should he try?

'Don't be so sure you're quicker than me,' Bragg said.

He was trying to talk himself into it.

'So far I been quick enough,' Cole said.

29

Bragg was silent for a moment. Then I could see him give up. He stood carefully with his hands apart and flat on the tabletop.

'This ain't the time,' he said.

'Um-hm.'

'Don't mean there won't be a time,' Bragg said.

'I see you are heeled and your boys there are heeled. I know you haven't had a chance to read the bylaws yet, so I'm gonna let it pass. But the bylaws say that it's illegal to carry guns inside town limits, so next time I'll have to disarm you and lock you up for a bit.'

Bragg's body stiffened. His shoulders seemed to hunch. He opened his mouth and closed it and stood for another moment. Then he turned without a word and walked out of the saloon. His ranch hands straggled after him.

CHAPTER 6

The woman got off the train in the morning carrying a big carpetbag, and walked slowly up the main street and into Café Paris, where Cole and I were having breakfast. I'd never been to Paris, but I'd read about it, and I was pretty sure there were no Café there like this one. One of the Chinamen who cooked there kept some chickens, so now and then they had some eggs on the menu. But today, like a lot of days, we were eating pinto beans and fried salt pork along with coffee and some sourdough biscuits. The biscuits were pretty tasty. The woman sat at a table near us and looked at the menu for a long time and finally ordered coffee and a biscuit.

'No sell,' the Chinaboy said.

'But they're on the menu,' she said.

'With breakfast.'

'But all I want is a biscuit.'

'No sell.'

Cole was wiping his plate with half a biscuit.

Without looking up, he said, 'Chin, sell her a biscuit.'

The Chinaboy looked at Cole for a moment, outraged at the impropriety of it.

'Boss say . . .'

'Sell her a biscuit,' Cole said again and looked up from his plate. The Chinaboy looked quickly away from Cole and went and brought the woman coffee and two biscuits on a plate. He added a pitcher of sorghum, to show that there was no ill will. The woman gave him twenty-five cents and looked across at Cole.

'Thank you,' she said.

Cole smiled at her.

'It was my pleasure,' he said.

She was a little travel-worn, but still good-looking, with a strong young body that her dress didn't hide. I could see her looking at the star on Cole's chest.

'Are you the sheriff here?' she said.

'City marshal,' Cole said. 'Virgil Cole. Big blond fella here is my deputy, Everett Hitch.'

'How do you do,' she said. 'Could you direct me to a clean, inexpensive hotel?'

'We only got one,' Cole said.

'Is it expensive?'

'Probably more than it should be, there being no other choices.'

'I only have a dollar,' she said.

Cole nodded.

'What's your name?' he said.

'Mrs French,' she said. 'Allison French.'

'You have a husband, Mrs French.'

'He died.'

'Sorry to hear that,' Cole said. 'You do any kind of work.'

'I play the organ,' she said. 'And the piano.'

'You're not a whore.'

'Don't be crude,' she said. 'No, I am not what you said.'

'No need fluffing your feathers about it,' Cole said. 'Don't see a lot of single women here that ain't whores.'

'Well, I'm one.'

'Sprightly thing,' Cole said to me.

I nodded. Cole was always improving himself, reading books, making lists of words, which he usually misused slightly.

'Will the hotel let me stay for a dollar?' Mrs French said.

Cole grinned.

'For as long as you'd like, Mrs French.'

She frowned.

'How can that be?' she said.

'Might hire you to play the piano, too,' Cole said. 'You think so, Everett?'

'I do,' I said.

'When you finish your breakfast,' Cole said, 'Everett here will escort you down and help you get settled.'

'Be my pleasure,' I said.

She finished her biscuit and slipped the other one into her carpetbag. Then she smiled and stood.

'Thank you very much, Mr Cole, for your kindness.'

'No trouble at all, Mrs French,' he said. 'Everett, you will speak with Mr Raines.'

'I will.'

Cole stood. Like all his movements, he seemed to go from sitting to standing without effort.

'Good,' Cole said. 'I hope to see you again, Mrs French.'

'Yes, Mr Cole, that would be nice.'

I picked up her carpetbag, and we walked down Main Street toward the hotel.

'You have freckles,' Mrs French said. 'Sandy hair and freckles.'

'Yes,' I said.

'I think that's so cute in a man.'

'Me, too,' I said.

I was more aware than I had been of the way her body moved under her skirts.

'How can Mr Cole be so sure that they will give me a room,' she said as we walked along the plank sidewalk.

I smiled. 'Because I'm going to tell the man who owns the place that Mr Cole wants them to.'

'Does Mr Cole always get what he wants?' she said.

'Pretty much,' I said.

CHAPTER 7

Mrs French played the piano very badly, but she played loud, and she was pretty and she smiled nice and wore dresses with a low neck and generated considerable heat and mostly nobody noticed. During her break she came over and sat at a table with me. I was drinking coffee.

I said, 'Care for a drink, Mrs French?'

'No, but I'll have some coffee with you,' she said. 'And, please, call me Allie.'

I nodded at Tilda and she came over with coffee for Allie, and a second cup for me.

'Have you known Mr Cole for long, Mr Hitch?'

'Call me Everett, and I'm pretty sure you should call Mr Cole Virgil.'

She smiled and looked down. The gesture looked practiced. Probably was.

'Have you known Virgil long, Everett?' she said.

'Yes.'

'And have you and he always been marshals here?'

'No. We just arrived couple weeks ago,' I said.

'Where were you before?'

'We been all over out here,' I said. 'Virgil gets

hired to settle things down in towns that need settling, and I go with him, and after the town gets settled, then we move on and find another town that needs settling.'

'Are you what they call "town tamers"?' she said.

'If you read those dime novels.'

'What do you call yourselves?' she said.

'Don't know as we ever have,' I said.

'Do you kill people?'

'Now and then,' I said.

'Many?'

Her eyes were up now and on me. It was always about the killing. I'd met a lot of women who were fascinated with the killing. They were horrified, too, but it was more than that.

'A few,' I said.

'And Virgil?'

'More than a few,' I said.

'What's it like?'

'It's like driving a nail,' I said.

'Like what?'

'Driving a nail, splitting firewood. It's work. It's quick.'

'No more than that?'

'Not after you've done it a couple times.'

'Do you like it?'

'Well, it's kind of clean and complete,' I said. 'You got him, he didn't get you.'

'But, if you feel that way,' she was frowning, thinking about it, interested, 'what's to prevent you from just killing anyone you feel like?'

'The law,' I said. 'Virgil always says, people obey the law, you don't have a reason to kill them.'

'Any law?'

'Don't get to complicating it,' I said.

'You know which law,' she said.

'We do.'

I liked how she was interested. How she hadn't decided what she thought before we started talking.

'How about the other people, the people you shoot?'

'Virgil always posts the laws,' I said. 'In any town we work.'

She drank her coffee, looking at me while she did.

'What if they kill you?'

'Hard thing to plan for,' I said.

'Do you think about it?'

'Try not to,' I said.

Neither of us said anything for a while. Tilda came over and poured us more coffee.

'I guess I disapprove,' Allie said.

I nodded.

'But I know I don't know enough about it, really,' she said. 'You seem like a nice man, and so does Mr Cole, Virgil.'

'I'm pretty nice,' I said. 'I'm not so sure 'bout Virgil.'

'Are either of you married?'

'I'm not,' I said.

'And, Mr . . . Virgil?'

'Not that I know about.'

37

'But you're his closet friend – wouldn't you know?'

'Virgil don't tell you much,' I said.

'Really? He seemed so talkative in the restaurant,' Allie said.

'Oh, he's talkative. Talks a lot of the time. He just don't tell you much.'

'Well,' she said. 'I'm going to ask him.'

CHAPTER 8

Appaloosa sat in a short valley. There were hills east and west, allowing the wind to funnel in from the north and rip through the town, swirling dust as high as the rooftops. From where Cole and I sat, drinking coffee on the front porch of the jail on a nice Sunday morning, we could see the valley rim to the west. Along the rim, two riders moved in slow silhouette.

'So,' Cole said, 'you been talking with Mrs French.'

'I have, Virgil.'

The riders on the rim paused and sat motionless, facing the town. It was a little far to see exactly who they were.

'What's she like to talk about?' Cole said.

'She was asking me a lot about you, Virgil.'

'She was. Was she asking in a liking way?'

'Wanted to know if you were married,' I said.

On the rim of the western slope, one of the horses nosed the flank of the other.

'She did, did she. By God. What'd you tell her.'

'Said I didn't know.'

'Well, hell, Everett,' Cole said. 'You see a wife around here?'

'I don't.'

'Then why the hell you tell her you didn't know.'

'Might have a wife in Silver City,' I said. 'Or Nogales, or Bisbee.'

'Had an Apache woman, lived with me once. Kinda like a wife, I guess. But there was never any words spoke over us or anything, and one day when I come home, she was gone.'

'Where?'

'Don't know.'

'You ever look for her?'

'I was going to,' Cole said. 'But then I got a job up in Durango, and I went up there. Never did know where she went. Back to the tribe, is most probable.'

The horsemen on the hill pulled their horses around and started off again, south, at a slow walk. One of them had rolled a cigarette, and even though they were a piece off, I could smell the tobacco.

'Well, Allie says she's going to ask you, so you might want to have an answer ready.'

He looked at me and frowned a little.

'She's going to ask me if I been married?'

'I think she's more interested in if you are presently married.'

'Hell, no, I'm not presently married.'

'She'll be pleased,' I said.

Cole nodded. He was looking at the horsemen on the rim.

'Been there since dawn,' Cole said.

'The riders?'

'Yep. Riding back and forth, looking at the town. There's two on the hill east of us.'

'Whaddya think?' I said.

'I think Mrs French might become exclusively interesting,' Cole said.

'Whaddya think about the men in the hills?' I said.

'I think you and me might want to ride up and see what they're doing up there.'

'Can I finish my coffee first?'

'You surely may,' Cole said.

CHAPTER 9

Cole and I fell in on each side of one of the ridge riders. The sun was behind us and made our three shadows stretch out long on the shaley trail.

'Howdy,' Cole said to the rider.

Without looking at either of us, the rider said, 'The town don't come out this far, Marshal.'

'By God,' Cole said, 'I believe you're right. I believe it ends just down there at the foot of the hill where that little wash runs.'

'So up here,' the rider said, 'you're just another cowboy with a gun.'

'You think that's right, Everett,' Cole said.

'I think no matter where you are, Cole, that you ain't just another cowboy with a gun.'

'That'd be my thought,' Cole said. 'So what are you doing riding round and round up here.'

'We ain't doing nothing wrong,' the rider said. 'And you ain't got no jurdiction up here.'

'"Jurdiction"?' Cole said and looked at me.

'I believe he means jurisdiction,' I said.

'I believe he does. And he's, by God, right about it.'

Cole smiled at the rider.

'So what are you doing riding round and round up here?'

The rider smirked a little.

'Just keepin' an eye on things.'

'On the town?' Cole said.

'Yeah.'

'For who?'

The rider shrugged. With an easy movement, Cole pulled the big Colt from its holster and hit the rider in the face with it. It knocked the rider out of his saddle, and by the time he hit the ground, the gun was back in its holster and Cole was leaning easily with his forearms resting on the horn of his saddle.

'You fucking broke my teeth,' the rider said, his hands to his face.

'Colt makes a heavy firearm,' Cole said. 'That's a fact. Who you riding for?'

The rider's nose was bleeding, and there was blood on his mouth.

'Bragg,' he said.

'And why's he want you riding round and round?'

'I don't know. He just told me to do it. Mr Bragg don't tell you why.'

'Think Bragg's attempting to frighten us, Everett?' Cole said.

'Be my guess,' I said.

'What's your name?' Cole said to the rider.

'Dean.'

'Well, Dean, you may as well head back to Mr Bragg and report that we ain't too frightened.'

'Mr Bragg ain't gonna like it that you hit me,' Dean said.

'I don't guess that you liked it all that much, yourself, Dean,' Cole said.

'That's right.'

'So you and Mr Bragg can, ah, co . . . Everett, what word am I trying for?'

'Commiserate,' I said.

'Commiserate,' Cole said. 'That's the word. You and Bragg can commiserate each other.'

Riding downhill toward town, I said to Cole, 'That fella wasn't actually doing nothing illegal.'

'He was annoying the hell out me,' Cole said.

'That's not illegal, Virgil.'

'No,' Cole said. 'It's personal.'

CHAPTER 10

When it was possible, Cole would sit with his one glass of whiskey and nurse it and watch Mrs French play the piano. She played with both hands, raising them high and bringing them down firmly with no difference that I could hear between the two. When she was through playing, she would come and sit with him. Cole wasn't expecting trouble today. I sat with them, too.

'So, tell me, Mr Cole,' she said. 'How long you been killing people for a living.'

'Call me Virgil,' he said.

He always said that and, to tease him, she always started out calling him Mr Cole.

'Of course, Virgil. How long?'

'I don't kill people for a living,' Virgil said. 'I enforce the law. Killing's sometimes a sorta side thing of that. . . . That ain't what I want to say. What am I aiming at, Everett?'

'By-product,' I said.

'Killing's sometimes a by-product,' Cole said.

'And you've never killed anybody except as a lawman?'

'Never,' Cole said. 'You gonna be killing people, you got to do it by the rules. Every man has his chance to surrender peaceable.'

'Is he telling me the truth, Everett?'

'Virgil always tells the truth,' I said.

'Nobody always tells the truth,' she said.

'Why not?' Cole said.

'Well,' Mrs French said, 'they, well, for heaven's sake, Virgil, they just don't.'

'Always thought the truth was simpler. Tell a man what you mean.'

'And a woman?' she said.

'A woman?'

'That's what I said.'

'Allie, I don't really remember telling a woman anything.'

'Virgil Cole,' she said. 'Are you telling me you've never had a woman?'

Cole's face got a little red.

'Well, hell, Allie, I don't think that's a thing I should be discussing with you.'

'But have you?' Allie said.

'Well, a' course,' he said. 'Assuredly, I have.'

'And did you never tell them anything?'

'Mostly I just did what we were there to do,' Virgil said.

His face was definitely red. She smiled at him, her head half turned away, looking at him sideways.

'And what was that?' she said.

It was like watching a cat play with prey.

There was a moment when nothing happened.

Then Virgil's face closed. It was over. He wasn't prey anymore. She had inched across the line. It wasn't smart to cross a line on Virgil. The problem was, it was never clear where the line was. Men had died making that mistake.

'We won't talk about this anymore,' he said.

He spoke softly, and his expression didn't change. But the redness left his face and something happened in his voice and in his eyes. It scared her.

'Virgil,' she said. 'I was just funning you.'

'I didn't enjoy it,' he said.

She sat frozen for a moment, then turned toward me.

'Everett,' she said. 'You ever lie?'

Her voice sounded stretched.

'All the time, Allie,' I said. 'All the time.'

'Well,' she said. 'Then I *understand* you.'

Virgil was quiet. There was no color in his face. Across the room, two men at the bar were in a contest to see who could drink a beer faster. I knew one of them, a pale man with soft hands who worked in a feed store. The other one was a teamster with a teamster's build: big belly from sitting all day on a wagon seat, and big muscles in his arms and shoulders from sawing on the reins of a six-mule rig over bad roads. The feed-store clerk was winning.

'You scrawny little bastard,' the teamster said in a loud voice. 'Where you putting it all? You ain't even pissed yet.'

47

The feed clerk laughed.

'Can't always tell somethin',' the clerk said, 'just by looking.'

'Goddamn,' the teamster said in his big voice. 'Two more, Willis. No fucking feed-store clerk is gonna back me down.'

Cole turned his head to look at them.

McDonough drew two glasses of beer. The men faced each other and each put a hand on his beer glass.

'Say when, Willis.'

'Now,' McDonough said, and the two men drank.

The feed clerk finished first.

'Shit!' the teamster said. 'Shit!'

Cole stood suddenly and walked to the bar.

'Shut up,' he said to the teamster.

The teamster looked startled.

'What's that, Marshal?'

'Shut your mouth and get out of here.'

'I ain't done nothing.' he said. 'Hell, Marshal, we're just drinking beer.'

Cole kicked him in the groin, and the teamster grunted and doubled over. The feed clerk ducked away as Cole hit the man. Cole was only middle-sized, and the teamster was big, but it was a slaughter. Cole hit him with both fists, one fist, then the other. He caught hold of the teamster's hair and slammed his face against the bar, and pulled it up and slammed it down again.

'Virgil,' I said.

The teamster was defenseless. Cole held him propped against the bar with his left shoulder while he hit him methodically with his right fist. Allie was watching. She seemed interested. I stepped over to them. The teamster's head lolled back. I could see that his eyes had rolled back. Blood and spittle trickled from his slack mouth. I got my arms around Cole's waist and picked him up off the ground and walked backward with him. He was still pumping his fist.

'Virgil,' I said. 'Virgil.'

He didn't fight me. He seemed unaware of me, as if his focus on the teamster was so enveloping that nothing else was real.

'Virgil,' I said.

He stopped moving his fist and held it, still cocked but still. I held on to him, listening to his breath snarl in and out of him. It felt as if there were something popping inside him, at his center.

'Virgil.'

His breath slowed. The popping eased.

'You can let go,' he said to me.

I relaxed a little but kept my arms around his waist.

'You can let go,' Virgil said.

I let go. He stood silently, his fist still cocked. Without Cole's shoulder to hold him, the teamster had sagged to the floor, his head twisted against the foot rail of the bar, his face covered with blood. Cole gazed at him steadily. I stood waiting. Willis McDonough had backed away down the bar and was polishing glasses at the far end. The feed clerk had disappeared. Everyone else in the room was motionless and silent. The only sound was Cole's breathing. Then I heard something else. It wasn't just Cole's breathing. Behind me. It was Allison French. She was breathing hard, too. We all held that way for a time that was probably much shorter then it seemed. Cole's breathing slowed. He still stared at the teamster.

'Loud-mouthed bastard,' he said and walked out of the bar.

The room stayed silent. I went back and sat down at the table with Allison. Her face was flushed, but her breathing, too, had slowed.

'My God,' she said.

'Virgil gets fractious when he's annoyed,' I said.

'But he let you pull him away.'

'Part of my duties.'

'He'll let you do that?'

'He wants me to,' I said.

'They didn't do anything,' Allison said.

'They were just drinking beer and having a good time. Why did he get so mad at the fat man?'

'He was mad at you,' I said.

CHAPTER 11

I was keeping company with a clean, dark-haired young whore named Katie Goode, who was a quarter Kiowa, a quarter Mex, and half some sort of travelin' Yankee. She and two other girls had a small house at the north end of town where they lived and conducted business. Katie had just finished conducting it with me, and we were lying in her bed in the back room.

'I heard the marshal almost killed Tub Gillis yesterday,' Katie said.

'Hit him a lot,' I said.

'I heard he done it for no reason,' Katie said.

'He had his reasons,' I said.

'I heard Tub wasn't doin' nothin' but drinking some beer with Bertie Frye.'

'Virgil was annoyed,' I said.

'At Tub?'

'Mrs French was raggin' him a little,' I said.

'Her,' Katie said.

'Her?'

'You heard me. You think she's such a sweet thing,' Katie said. 'All you men. Girls know better.

She should move up to the north end with the rest of us.'

'You think she's a whore?'

'She's wiggling her sweet ass for money just like the rest of us.'

'Except you,' I said. 'With me.'

'Of course, Everett.'

'How do you know about Mrs French?'

'I go in there. She sees me, she looks like she's looking at a bug. But I see the way she is. She's looking to get those hooks of hers into some man. Might be Marshal Cole.'

'He's taken with her,' I said.

'How about you, Everett? Are you taken with her?'

'I don't think that would be a good idea,' I said.

'Not a good idea what?'

'To be taken with her,' I said.

''Cause of Marshal Cole?'

'Nope.'

'So you don't think she's such a prize cow, either, do you,' Katie said.

'I don't know about her,' I said. 'But I wish Virgil weren't quite so taken up with her.'

'She have a husband?'

'She says so. Says he died.'

'Probably fucked him to death, be my guess,' Katie said.

'Not a bad way to go,' I said.

'You like the way she plays the piano?'

'No.'

'Me neither.'

'I don't want you sayin' nothing to Virgil about this,' I said.

'I don't talk to him. I'm scared of him.'

'Yes,' I said. 'Virgil can be a touch intimidatin'. And I don't think he's had as much experience with women as I have. But he's got the right to fall for any woman he wants.'

'You got a lot of experience with women, Everett?'

'From Fort Worth to Cheyenne,' I said. 'I got more notches on my pecker than a handsaw.'

'Well, you learned one thing good,' Katie said.

'I hope so.'

'You can do it again, for free,' Katie said, 'if you want to.'

'I believe I do,' I said.

'Then go right ahead, Everett.'

'I believe I will.'

CHAPTER 12

The teamster had a room at a place on Front Street, behind the livery. He was in his drawers when I went in, lying on an unmade bed against the wall. The room was hot. There was some air coming through the open window, but the air was hot, too. His face was badly swollen. One eye was shut up tight. The bruising had begun to darken all over him. When I came in, he sat up stiffly on the bed. His torso was bruised. I put a bottle of whiskey on the table in front of the window.

'Somethin' to sip on,' I said. 'Kill the pain.'

'Whatcha want?' he said.

His voice was strained through his swollen mouth. It was hard for him to speak. The one eye he could see out of looked frightened. It's easy to be frightened when you're hurt.

'Just want to see how you're holdin' up,' I said. 'Bring you the bottle.'

The teamster opened the bottle and drank from the neck. He flinched when the whiskey went in. His mouth was probably cut up inside. And he shuddered when he swallowed. But as soon as he got the swallow down, he took another drink.

'How come he done that?' he said.

'Virgil was mad,' I said. 'You was there.'

'I wasn't doing nothin'.'

'Doctor seen you?' I said.

'Says my nose is broke.'

'Pack it with lint?'

'Ya. How come the marshal done that?'

'No accountin' for things, sometimes,' I said. 'Virgil says to tell you he's very sorry 'bout it. Asked me to give you some money, pay the doctor, maybe buy some more whiskey.'

I put some money on the table next to the bottle. The teamster squinted at it.

'He shouldn't a done that,' the teamster mumbled. 'He gimme no warning.'

'Coulda been worse. Coulda shot you.'

'He shouldn't a.'

'He knows that,' I said. 'Why he sent me over.'

'Why didn't he come?'

'Virgil don't do things like that,' I said.

'He don'?'

'No.'

'Why not?'

'He's Virgil Cole,' I said.

The teamster nodded, and it hurt, and he stopped and took another pull on the bottle.

'Whiskey might help,' he said. 'Can you get me 'nother bottle?'

'I will,' I said. 'You need any food?'

'Jesus, no,' the teamster said.

'Anything else?'

'No. Yes. Whiskey.'

He drank some more.

'Help?' I said.

'Maybe,' he said. 'Maybe help.'

'I'll go get you another bottle,' I said. 'And I'll stop now and then, see how you are.'

'Thanks.'

'You rest up. When you can eat, I'll bring you something.'

'Thanks.'

'Marshal and me are both real sorry,' I said, 'that this happened.'

'Me, too,' the teamster said.

CHAPTER 13

I was in the marshal's office on First Street when Phil Olson came in. It was a hot day, and Olson's pink face was damp.

'Cole around?' he said.

'Walkin' the town,' I said.

'We need to talk.'

'Talk to me,' I said.

'Really should be him,' Olson said. 'It's about that teamster he busted up.'

'Might be better you talked with me about that,' I said. 'Virgil can get grouchy sometimes when he done something he wishes he hadn't.'

'You think he wishes he hadn't?'

'He does,' I said.

'What happened?' Olson said.

'Virgil was kind of riled,' I said. 'Teamster was a handy target.'

'He wasn't even riled at Mr Gillis?'

'That his name?'

'Yes. His employer came and spoke to me about it.'

'I been to visit him.' I said.

'Mr Gillis?'

57

'Yes.'

'How is he?'

'Lotta swelling,' I said. 'He'll recover.'

'My God. Is he going to sue us?'

'Us?'

'The town. Mr Cole is a town employee. Mr Gillis's employer said he was going to advise him to sue the town.'

'I'm not so sure he can do that,' I said. 'When Judge Callison comes around, you oughta ask him.'

'Well, whether he can or not,' Olson said, 'we can't have our law officers beating people half to death for no good reason.'

I leaned back in my chair and shifted my hips a little so my gun wouldn't dig into my side, and put my feet up on the desk and looked up at the tan-painted pressed-tin ceiling for a time without saying anything while I collected my thoughts.

'Thing is,' I said, 'you got to see Virgil from all sides, so to speak. Takes a certain kind of man to be Virgil Cole. You hire him to do your gun work for you because you ain't that kind of man. No need feelin' bad about it. Most people ain't that kind of man. But Virgil is, and what makes him that kind of man can't always just be lit up and blowed out like a candle.'

'What he did was crazy,' Olson said.

'Virgil is crazy. You think a man ain't crazy will make his living as a gun hand? You ever been in a gunfight?'

Olson didn't say anything.

'You ever?' I said again.

'No.'

'Gun's right there looking at you, hammer's back. You see the snouts of the bullets peeking out of the cylinder like reptiles in a hole. Most people can't stand up to that. Most people start to feel their intestines loosen. Virgil don't. Virgil been doing that for years, and he ain't never backed down, and he ain't never run, and he ain't never lost,' I said. 'Because he's a little crazy. And crazy is what it takes.'

'Don't give him the right to go around busting up innocent people,' Olson said.

'No,' I said. 'It don't. And mostly, innocent people don't get busted up. And if they do, every once in a while, it's because of who Virgil Cole is, and what he is, and you hired him to be Virgil Cole. You hired the craziness.'

Olson was silent for a time, thinking about what I said. I kept looking at the tin ceiling.

'You're not crazy,' Olson said finally.

'Maybe, maybe not,' I said. 'But whatever I am, I ain't Virgil Cole.'

'But you been working with him for years. I saw you shoot that man, Bragg's man, in the bar.'

'I ain't Virgil,' I said. 'I'm his helper.'

'And that makes a difference?' Olson said.

'All the difference,' I said.

'But,' Olson said. 'Cole works for us. I feel we have the right to tell him when he's done something wrong.'

'You got the right,' I said.

'But you think we shouldn't.'

'I think you shouldn't.'

'What would happen?' Olson said.

He wasn't combative. He seemed more curious than anything.

'Make Virgil peevish,' I said.

'What would he do.'

'Hard to be sure,' I said. 'But making Virgil peevish is never good.'

'But I can talk to you about it.'

'I tole you. I ain't Virgil.'

'You're his helper.'

'I am.'

'I'm not sure I understand,' Olson said.

'No,' I said. 'I'm not sure you do, either.'

CHAPTER 14

Since Virgil had taken up with Allie French, they liked to sleep in. And I usually had breakfast alone at Café Paris, or, if I wanted something better than fried salt pork and refried pinto beans, at the Boston House. I was at the Boston House, smoking a cigar and drinking coffee after breakfast, when Allie and Virgil came down the hotel stairs and into the dining room. Allie came over and gave me a kiss on the top of my head and sat down at the table. Virgil sat beside her.

'Morning,' he said.

I said good morning. Tilda came over and poured coffee. They consulted on the menu and decided on pancakes.

'I went over and seen that teamster,' I said to Virgil.

'He all right?' Virgil said.

'He will be, soon's the swelling goes down.'

'Good.'

That was as close as Virgil could come to admitting anything about his assault on Mr Gillis. I knew it, and knew it was heartfelt.

'He might not be all right if Everett hadn't pulled you off him,' Allie said.

'I know,' Virgil said.

Which was as close as he was ever going to get to admitting that he was glad I'd done it.

'I gave him some money,' I said. 'Help him out while he can't work.'

Virgil nodded. It would never occur to him that he should reimburse me, and it would never occur to me that I should ask. It was part of being Virgil's helper. Allie was watching both of us. She took a delicate sip of her coffee and made a delicate shudder to show us that she was a lady and not made for strong brew.

'I swear,' she said. 'Sometimes I sit here and watch you two grunt at each other, and have the feeling that there's a whole conversation going on that I don't even hear.'

I grinned at her.

'No,' I said. 'We're just grunting, Allie.'

'Well,' she said, 'whatever it is, I just always feel left out.'

'For God's sake, Allie,' Cole said. 'We ain't talking about nothing. We don't have that much to talk about.'

A tall cowboy with a big hat came into the dining room and waited for his eyes to adjust, and looked around the room. He saw us and studied us for a minute. I saw Cole shift a little in his chair so that his gun hand was loose and free.

'You know him,' Cole said.

'No.'

'Know who?' Allie said.

'He heeled?' Cole said.

'Right-hand pants pocket,' I said.

'Are you talking about that tall man?' Allie said.

Allie was on my right. I hitched my chair a little away from her, so that my right hand was free. Virgil stood and turned so he was in front of Allie, between her and the tall cowboy. The cowboy came toward us.

'You the marshal?' he said.

'Virgil Cole.'

'Name's Whitfield,' he said. 'I need to talk.'

'That'll be fine,' Virgil said, 'but I need to take that iron you got in your pocket.'

'You want my gun?'

'Just while you're in town,' Virgil said. ''Gainst the law in town.'

Whitfield reached to his right-hand pocket.

'Very slow,' I said.

'This your deputy?' Whitfield said.

'Everett Hitch,' Cole said. 'Hold it by the barrel.'

Whitfield handed it butt-first to Cole. It was a pocket gun, hammerless and nickel-plated. It looked like a .32.

'What's this for?' Cole said, 'shooting women?'

'It'll keep somebody off ya,' Whitfield said. 'If they're close.'

Cole put the gun on the table next to me. Allie sat very still, watching everything that happened. She seemed to like it.

'Have a seat,' Cole said. 'Maybe some coffee?'

'Coffee be good,' Whitfield said.

Whitfied took his hat off and put it on the table. He looked at Allie.

'This the missus?' he said.

Cole's face colored a little.

'No,' Cole said. 'This is Mrs French.'

The cowboy said, 'Pleased to meet you.'

'Like wise,' Allie said. 'I'm sure.'

Tilda brought some more coffee. Nobody said anything. Allie waited, interested. Whitfield was silent. Finally, Cole said, 'Allie, I got to talk to this fella alone.'

'Oh? Well, certainly, Virgil. I've got to do my piano exercises anyway.'

She stood.

'Nice meeting you,' she said to Whitfield.

'My pleasure, ma'am,' Whitfield said.

Allie walked off toward the piano beyond the bar, and sat at it. She opened the cover and began to play some sort of musical exercises that didn't sound much different than when she really played.

'I used to be a deputy here,' Whitfield said.

Cole was quiet.

'Worked with Jack Bell.'

Cole nodded.

'I knew Jack,' Cole said.

'Went up to Bragg's place with him one day to arrest coupl'a Bragg's men.'

Cole nodded.

'Bragg wouldn't give 'em up,' Whitfield said. 'They was too many, but Jack, he . . .'

'I know what happened,' Cole said.

'Was me,' Whitfield said. 'And Dave Long, and Jack.'

Cole nodded.

'They was too many,' Whitfield said.

'I know,' Cole said. 'And they shot Bell and the other deputy and you skedaddled.'

Whitfield nodded.

'You know it happened,' he said.

'Know it, can't prove it,' Cole said.

'No witnesses,' Whitfield said.

'Un-huh.'

'I run off like a yellow dog,' Whitfield said.

'No reason to die for nothing,' Cole said.

'But I come back.'

Cole nodded.

'And I'll be your witness.'

'Good,' Cole said. 'Care to go with us?'

'Go with you?'

'When we go to apprehend Mr Bragg,' Cole said.

Whitfield shook his head.

'Can't,' he said. 'I . . . I dunno, it busted me up inside when Jack got killed and I run. I . . . can't do gun work no more.'

'But you'll testify,' Cole said.

'I will.'

'With Bragg looking right at you,' Cole said.

'I will.'

'I don't want to go up there,' Cole said, 'and

65

shoot up a lotta people, and get Bragg into court, and have you dry up and blow away.'

'I won't.'

'You won't relinquish on your testimony.'

'I'll say what I seen,' Whitfield said.

Cole was silent. He looked at me. I nodded. Whitfield saw the nod.

'That's right,' he said. 'I'll stand. I can't do gun work no more, but I can say what I seen, and I'll stand and say it.'

'I got your word on that?' Cole said.

'You do.'

'All right,' Cole said. 'Everett and me will go up and apprehend him.'

CHAPTER 15

'Alone?' Raines said.

'Me and Everett,' Cole said.

'But that's all?' Raines said. 'You two alone?'

'Me and Everett,' Cole said again.

'Bragg's got forty gun hands up there.'

'Twenty-five,' Cole said.

'You say that like it made a difference.'

'Makes a difference of, ah, how much, Everett?'

'Fifteen,' I said.

'It's still so many,' Raines said.

'Specimens I've seen so far don't enliven me much,' Cole said.

'We could get a posse up, deputize a bunch of us.'

'Coulda done that 'fore you hired us, Abner,' Cole said.

'You don't want help?'

'No. I got help, I gotta worry about them. They get in trouble, I got to get them out. Better just me and Everett.'

I thought Raines looked relieved.

'Well, you say so, Virgil. It's your kinda work, I guess.'

'It is,' Cole said.

Raines stood and walked out of the marshal's office. He turned left on the boardwalk and disappeared.

'You got a plan?' I said to Cole.

'Well, we ain't going to go riding in there bold as brass,' Cole said. 'Like Jack Bell done.'

'I hear Bell was good,' I said.

'He was. He was good with a gun. Worked a lot of tough towns.'

'Overconfident?' I said.

'Be my surmise,' Cole said. 'Thought he could back Bragg down. Thought they wouldn't shoot lawmen.'

'You think you could back Bragg down?' I said.

'Just me and him?' Cole said. 'Just the two of us? I could back him a ways. And then he wouldn't back no farther.'

'You know this?'

'Sure.'

'How?'

'Been doing this a long time, Everett. Ain't just gun work. Gotta think about men, too.'

'Which would, I guess, be one reason you're here and Jack Bell ain't,' I said.

'Yep,' Cole said and nodded his head. 'That'd be a reason. You'd be another.'

I opened my mouth and closed it and sat. I didn't know what to say. Cole had never been quite so straight with me about what I was worth. I sort of smiled to myself.

'What you smilin' about,' Cole said.

'I caught myself thinking,' I said. 'And what I was thinking was that you was right.'

Cole didn't comment.

'So,' he said. 'What we got to do next is drift on up there and look at Bragg's layout.'

CHAPTER 16

Bragg's ranch was on an upland meadow with a stream. There were some trees along the stream, and a small herd of beef cattle grazed in the grass under their shade.

'Pretty place,' Cole said.

We were sitting our horses behind the ranch, on a hill that looked over it. We could see across it to Appaloosa in the sere valley below. Someone spotted us there, and several men gathered on the porch of the big ranch house and looked up at us. I saw Bragg was taller than anyone else.

'No cover,' I said.

'Nope, nothin' much,' Cole said. 'Maybe a little among them trees.'

'For how long?' I said.

'Long as it would take them to send some people around behind us,' Cole said.

'No real way to slide in on them without them knowing it,' I said.

'Depends how hard they sleep,' Cole said.

'Don't think they got a nighthawk?' I said.

'If they did, depend on how hard he listened.'

'There's a way to find out,' I said.

'Un-huh.'

''Cept now they seen us,' I said. 'Makes it likely they'll be more careful.'

'Don't matter,' Cole said. 'We'll expedite us a way.'

''Spose we will,' I said.

Cole was silent, looking down at the gray, weathered ranch buildings. There was a barn with a corral. Some horses stood quietly in the corral, the way horses do, heads down, doing nothing. There was a bunkhouse on the other side of the barn, with a cookshack angling off it. There were two outhouses: a big one near the bunkhouse, and another smaller one near the ranch house.

'We'll ride on back to town,' Cole said. 'Give them time to relax a little, and maybe two, three nights from now, we'll ride on back up and see what happens at night.'

The horses knew the way back, and they moved almost without guidance. Behind us, as we moved downhill toward Appaloosa in the punch bowl, half a dozen riders from Bragg's outfit sat their horses on the hilltop where we'd been and watched us go.

I said, 'Law's a little thin on this, Virgil.'

'Don't see why. Bragg killed the marshal. Now I'm the marshal and I can prove he done it.'

'There'll be twenty of them all swear he didn't.'

'That ain't up to me,' Cole said. 'That's for the trial.'

'Ain't even sure we got jurisdiction,' I said. 'We city lawmen. Bragg might not even be in the city.'

'He's close enough,' Cole said. 'He killed Jack Bell.'

71

'Might be able to prove Jack Bell got killed up there. Hard to prove exactly who done it.'

'Everett,' Cole said. 'You gettin' gun-shy.'

'Just examining the situation, Virgil.'

'Pretty soon you'll be telling me Jack Bell ain't dead.'

'Truth is, Virgil, we don't know that he is.'

'Well, where the hell is he?'

'Oh, I'm sure he's dead. But we don't know it, you understand, we only been told it.'

'What's the difference,' Cole said. 'You know it. I know it. You ever read this man Ralph Emerson?'

'Some sort of philosopher,' I said.

'"What I must do concerns me, not what people think."'

'He said that?'

'He did,' Cole said

'He might not'a been talking about the Appaloosa marshal,' I said.

'I knew Jack Bell,' Cole said.

Cole's horse tossed his head and skittered a couple of quick steps sideways. I didn't know if Virgil asked him, or if something had caught his notice. Didn't matter. I knew there was no point talking to Virgil anymore. He was going to do what he was going to do. All I could do is trail along with him and keep him from getting back shot.

'Everything good with you and Allie,' I said when I got beside him again.

'Lovely,' Cole said. 'She's a lovely woman, and everything's lovely between us.'

'She can rile you a little,' I said.

'She's playful,' Cole said. 'It don't rile me at all.'

'Didn't have nothin' to do with you pounding on the teamster, Gillis.'

Cole didn't answer. It was as if he hadn't heard.

'Sorta thought it mighta had somethin' to do with you bein' annoyed at Allie.'

'She's a very lovely lady,' Cole said. 'Very lovely.'

CHAPTER 17

We looked at Bragg's spread for half of a brightly moonlit night. We rode up there in the afternoon another day. Always we sat, looking down at the ranch in plain sight. One day we rode up real early, while it was still dark.

Dawn was just starting to streak the eastern sky when we got there and held up on the hill above the ranch, where they could see us.

'Might be more clever,' I said to Cole, 'if we was to sneak a little.'

'No need to sneak,' Cole said. 'We're the law.'

'Might be more clever if we got him to come into town and jumped him there.'

'I'm going to take him out here at his ranch and bring him in like Jack Bell was going to do.'

'Because?'

Cole didn't answer. He sat his horse, looking at the ranch.

'You close with Bell?' I said.

'Not so much,' Cole said.

'But he was city marshal and now you're city marshal.'

Cole nodded.

'And this is all about the law?'

'Killing a city marshal ain't legal,' Cole said.

'Ralph philosopher fella say that?'

Cole grinned.

'Virgil Cole,' he said.

We sat some more. I had looked at the ranch so much that I felt as though I'd worked there. Smoke began to wisp up out of the cookshack. A couple of hands stumbled down to the big outhouse. Somebody lit a lamp in the main house, and then Bragg came out shirtless with his pants on and walked to the small outhouse.

'Now, you see that,' Cole said. 'They got them a big privy down there, probably a four-holer, for the hands. And Bragg got his own personal one, nearer the house.'

I nodded. Cole never talked just to be talking, though when he did talk, he seemed to ramble. That was mostly he wasn't talking, he was thinking out loud and new thoughts occurred to him in the process. For actual talking, if it wasn't for me prodding him, he might not talk at all.

'All we got to do,' Cole said, 'is get hold of him. Once we got him, it don't matter how many gun hands he got.'

I nodded.

'See how them orange Osage come off at a angle from the cottonwoods along the stream?'

I nodded just to be doing something. Cole wasn't really talking to me.

'Probably ran it up there for a windbreak in the winter,' Cole said. 'Ain't enough of it planted to fence off cattle.'

'Too short a span,' I said, just to be saying something.

'If we was to set in there behind that Osage orange, with an extra saddle horse, and maybe we be there before the sun's up. Then we wait, and when Bragg comes down to use the privy, we move in close and take him.'

'What about the night rider?' I said.

'He'll be looking for us up on the hill,' Cole said.

'That's why we let them see us up there all that time,' I said. 'That's where they'll expect us to be.'

Cole paid no attention to me.

'Before or after?' I said.

'Before or after what?'

'Before he goes into the privy, or after he comes out.'

'After,' Cole said. 'I don't want to get pissed on.'

CHAPTER 18

There was a night rider. I couldn't see him, but I heard his horse blow from the direction of the hill. We had a livery horse, saddled, on a lead. We were on foot, leading the horses as we went in the darkness down along the row of trees. We stopped fifty feet away from the privy. It was still too dark to see, but we could smell it. I took the shotgun off my saddle. We tied the horses loosely to one of the hedge apples. And we stood. Somewhere far off, some prairie chickens boomed. The sky in the east began to lighten. A rooster crowed. We stood. I smelled wood smoke. The sky was pale now in the east. We could see the outhouse on the other side of the trees. Uphill toward where we always sat and watched, I could see the night rider moving across the slope halfway up.

In back of us, I could hear the bunkhouse's door open, as some of the hands went to their privy. I smelled coffee mixed with the wood smoke. Then bacon. Beside me, Cole murmured.

'Here he comes.'

I didn't hear anything. But I was used to that.

Cole always heard things sooner than I did and saw things sooner. I heard his footsteps. I heard the door to the privy open and swing shut. Then nothing.

Cole gestured toward the privy. I slipped through the trees and along one side of it. Cole went around the back to the other side. And we waited. When Bragg came out, we were on either side of him. Cole took a handful of Bragg's hair in his left hand and pressed the barrel of his Colt against Bragg's temple.

'Not a fucking sound,' he said softly.

I pressed the two barrels of the eight-gauge up under Bragg's chin. And packed close together, we walked back behind the Osage orange trees toward the horses. When we reached the horses, Cole let go of Bragg's hair.

'Mount up,' Cole said.

I eased off on the shotgun so Bragg could climb into the saddle. It made him a little braver.

'You can't do this,' he said.

'Can or can't,' Cole said. 'Won't make no difference to you. First time there's trouble, we kill you.'

Bragg's mount had no reins. The horse was on a lead, tethered to my saddle horn.

'Ride,' Cole said.

We moved down the line of trees, walking the horses. Cole rode on one side of Bragg and I road on the other with the eight-gauge resting across my saddle, pointing at Bragg. As we cleared the trees near the stream, the nighthawk spotted us and came down the hill at a gallop, shouting.

'Pull the horses in tight as we can,' Cole said. 'Make it hard to shoot us without shooting Bragg.'

We kept walking. By the time we neared the river, there were half a dozen horsemen coming toward us on the run.

'Put that brush cutter right up against him, if you would, Everett,' Cole said. 'Being sure that it's cocked.'

It was too hard to ride tight and keep the gun under Bragg's chin. I settled for pressing it into his side. We reached the river and moved toward the ford. At the ford, there were maybe twelve riders with guns.

'Tell them to let us pass,' Cole said.

Bragg was silent. We kept walking toward the ford. Holding the reins in his left hand, Cole drew his Colt, cocked it, and placed it carefully against Bragg's cheekbone. If it began, Bragg didn't have a prayer. We were bunched together, so we were barely more than a single target. Cole had a gun against Bragg's face. The two barrels of my shotgun were digging into his side.

'What you want us to do, Mr Bragg?' one of the riders said.

'Hold off, Vince,' Bragg said.

His voice was hoarse and strained. Vince was hatless, and there was a pale line on his forehead. He was smallish, with big hands and a big blond moustache stained with something. Tobacco juice, maybe. Maybe coffee. He sat on a blue roan gelding that looked like a runner, and he held a

Winchester in one hand, the butt resting on his thigh. We kept walking our horses toward the ford. The sun was up now, still low, and the western edge of the sky still dark purple, but everyone could see clearly.

As we reached them, Bragg's riders parted, half to one side, half to the other, and the three of us rode slowly between them. No one spoke. I could feel the pressure of the silence all through me. The only sound was the horses' hooves and their breathing, and the creak of saddle leather. The horses hesitated at the water, but Cole and I kicked ours forward and the three of us went in. The line of riders that had parted to let us through closed ranks behind us and turned toward the river. It was as if I could feel them looking at us. It made the muscles across my back tighten. The water was higher than the stirrups; my boots were wet and the lower half of my pants. The river smelled very fresh in the early-morning air. The horses climbed the far bank, and we stood for a moment on the other side. Without lowering his gun, Cole turned in the saddle and looked back across the river.

'Tell them not to follow,' he said to Bragg.

Again, Bragg was silent. I could see the flush of redness on his cheekbones.

'I'd like you dead, Bragg,' Cole said quietly. 'I'm taking you in legal, like a law officer, but if you attempt to escape or impede me in my duty, I got every right to shoot you dead, and no one will say no.'

'If you kill me,' Bragg said, 'then there ain't no reason for my men not to chase you down and kill you.'

'If they can,' Cole said. 'Either way, won't make no difference to you.'

Bragg was silent. Cole was silent. The horses stood quietly, tossing their heads every once in a while for reasons of their own.

'Tell 'em not follow us,' Cole said to Bragg, 'or I'll shoot you dead right here. Right now.'

Again, there was silence. Cole's face showed nothing. I could hear Bragg's breathing. He looked at me.

'You?' he said.

'Both barrels,' I said.

He turned his head slowly away from Cole's gun and looked back at the line of riders back across the river.

'Vince,' he hollered.

'Yessir, Mr Bragg.'

'Don't follow us. You understand.'

'They making you say that, Mr Bragg?'

'They are. But I mean it. Stay put.'

'You say so, Mr Bragg.'

We moved the horses forward again. A half mile from the ranch, Cole holstered his Colt, and I slid the shotgun back in the saddle scabbard.

'Do hope you'll make a run for it,' Cole said to Bragg. 'Save us all a lot of time and trouble.'

'I'm riding in with you,' Bragg said.

Which he did.

CHAPTER 19

There were two jail cells along the right wall of the marshal's office as you entered. Both cell doors stood open.

'You prefer one to another?' Cole said when we brought Bragg in.

'Don't matter,' Bragg said. 'I won't be here long.'

'Circuit judge don't come through for two and a half weeks, if he's on time,' Cole said.

'I won't be here long,' Bragg said again.

He went into the first cell and pulled the door shut behind him. I locked it and took the key. The rest of the office was very plain: a stove for winter, a big old table that Cole used for a desk, two straight chairs against the wall opposite the cells, a spittoon in the corner, and a wooden water bucket and dipper sitting on one of the chairs. Bragg sat on the cot in the cell and looked at us.

'Need to be on him all the time,' Cole said to me. 'Round the clock.'

I nodded.

'I'll stay here,' Cole said. 'You go down, get something to eat, and come back. Bring him some.'

'I'll be at the Chinaman's,' I said. 'Won't take long.'

Cole sat down at the big table and laid his Winchester on it. I leaned my shotgun against the wall next to Cole and handed him the key to Bragg's cell. He tossed it on the table, put his feet up, and tilted his chair back. I went to lunch.

When I came back with boiled beef and navy beans on a tin plate for Bragg, Cole was in the same position. As far as I could tell, he hadn't moved. Except that his eyes were open, I'd have thought he was asleep. There was a small pass-through in the cell door. I passed the food in. Bragg took it silently and sat back down and set it on the cot beside him.

'I'm goin' to have lunch with Allie,' Cole said. 'Be back before suppertime. Any trouble, you fire off a couple of rounds and I'll hear you.'

''Less you're riding at a hard gallop,' I said.

Cole stopped at the doorway and turned.

'We known each other a long time, Everett,' Cole said. 'But I don't care for them kinds of remarks, 'bout Allie French.'

'No, and you shouldn't,' I said. 'I apologize.'

Cole nodded.

'Apology accepted,' Cole said. 'You meant no harm.'

He paused for a moment on his way out. Then he gestured for me to join him and stepped out onto the boardwalk. I went out with him and left the door open.

'I figure,' he said to me quietly, 'that we're going to need to keep an eye on Whitfield.'

'We'll need him,' I said, 'when the judge gets here.'

'And we have to watch Bragg,' Cole said.

'Maybe we can keep him a secret,' I said.

Cole shook his head.

'Town's too small,' he said. 'Half the people in town already know he's back.'

'We could put him in the other cell,' I said. 'Then one of us could watch them both.'

Cole was quiet for a minute.

'Yes, we'll do that,' he said. 'I'll bring him down soon as I've seen Allie.'

He turned without saying anything else and started toward the hotel. I went back into the office and sat in the chair he'd vacated and turned and looked at Bragg. He looked back. Neither of us said anything. He hadn't touched the food. After a while I put my feet up on the desk and tilted the chair back the same as Cole had and tilted my hat down and closed my eyes and had a nap.

CHAPTER 20

We kept Whitfield in one cell and Bragg in the other, the only difference being that Bragg's cell was locked. Bragg spent much of his time looking at Whitfield like a hangman looking at a felon. It made Whitfield nervous, but there was nothing to be done. He spent a lot of time sitting outside the office with me, watching whatever was happening on Main Street. When I sat out there, I left the office door open and held the eight-gauge across my lap.

'When's that judge coming through here, now?' Whitfield said.

'Ten more days.'

'You think they'll put Bragg in jail?'

'Ain't my department,' I said.

'What happens to me after the trial.'

'You ride on back to wherever you rode on to the first time,' I said.

'You think they'll try to get me?'

'You ain't sleeping in the jail for comfort,' I said.

'Even after the trial?'

'Straight on,' I said. 'We'll ride you out away,

give you a head start, and you can disappear. You done it before.'

'Why the hell am I doing this?' Whitfield said.

'The right thing to do?'

'Get my ass shot,' Whitfield said. 'That's what I'll do.'

From where I sat, I could glance back through the open door and see Bragg's cell. He was lying on his bunk, staring at the ceiling.

'Me 'n Virgil will prevent that,' I said.

'I run off once,' Whitfield said.

Across the street, two women in bonnets and long dresses walked past. One of them walked with a beguiling wiggle. We both watched until she turned into McKenzie's Store. And then we both watched the store, waiting for her to come out.

'I run off before,' Whitfield said. 'I couldn't stop myself. I seen Jack go down and the other deputy – hell, I don't even remember his name – and I was running 'fore I even knew it.'

'It can happen,' I said.

'Ever happen to you?'

An eight-horse team pulled a lumber wagon past us, kicking up the dust in the street. I watched them go past.

'Did it?'

'Did it what?' I said.

'Ever happen to you?'

'You mean did I ever run off in the heat of battle?' I said.

'Yeah.'

I shook my head.

'Nope, can't say I ever did.'

'I done it.'

'I know,' I said. 'And I ain't saying I won't. Men break when they break, mostly.'

The two women came out of McKenzie's carrying parcels. They headed back the way they had come. The one with the wiggle was walking closest to the street. Her dress was tight.

'Good-looking ass,' Whitfield said.

'I noticed that, too,' I said.

We watched her move away from us. At the corner of Second Street, she glanced back over her shoulder at us and then turned the corner and disappeared.

'I'm bettin' Virgil Cole never run.'

'Be a good bet,' I said. 'I honestly don't think Virgil's ever even been afraid.'

'What kind of man ain't afraid,' Whitfield said.

'I don't know,' I said. 'I been with Virgil Cole a long time, and I don't know much of anything about him.'

'You ever afraid?'

'I am.'

'But you don't run.'

'Not yet,' I said.

'I was all right with the drunks and the sodbusters,' Whitfield said. 'But first time it got tough, I run.'

'And you're afraid you'll do it again,' I said.

A lone rider came around the corner from First Street at the far end of town and began to ride down Main Street. Tilda scuttled past us on her way to work, furtive as a small desert animal.

'I guess maybe I am,' Whitfield said. 'I hope I don't. I don't want to live like that all the rest of my life.'

The lone rider came closer. He was smallish, with big hands and a thick, unsightly blond moustache. He was chewing tobacco. Now and then he would lean out in the saddle so as to spit and not get it on the horse. I recognized him. It was Bragg's foreman. He stopped when he came opposite the marshal's office and sat his horse and looked at us.

I nodded.

He didn't respond.

I said, 'Howdy, Vince.'

He didn't say anything. He looked at me briefly, and at Whitfield for a long time. Then he surveyed the office and the street and the buildings on each side of the office.

I could hear Whitfield's breathing.

Vince leaned out away from the horse and spit his chew into the street. Then he straightened, took a large plug out of his shirt pocket and a jackknife out of his pants pocket, and cut off a chunk and fed it off the knife blade into his mouth. He folded the plug back up in its paper, closed the jackknife, and put it back in his pants. He sat straight now in his saddle, both hands resting on the saddle horn, and chewed the fresh cut of tobacco until it felt right to him. Then, without a word, he turned the horse slowly and rode on down Main Street and turned out of sight onto First.

Beside me, I heard Whitfield exhale.

'Know him?' I said.

'No, but he's a gun hand,' Whitfield said. 'I ain't seen 'em like you have. But I seen enough to know.'

'Yeah,' I said. 'He's a gun hand.'

'He with Bragg?' Whitfield said.

'Un-huh.'

Whitfield didn't say anything else. We both sat quiet. But I could hear the breath go in and out of him, and I could hear him swallow.

CHAPTER 21

I spent more time guarding Bragg and protecting Whitfield than Cole did. Cole was building a house, and he spent a lot of time at it while I minded the store. He and Allie had picked out a lot on the corner of First Street and Front Street, which put them at the very edge of town and would give them a back-window view of the easy upslope of the hills. It was raining one day when Cole came into the marshal's office, his hat pulled down, the collar up on his slicker.

'Allie's been chewin' on me like a young dog,' Cole said. 'I don't spend enough time with her. All I do is be a marshal and sit around with you, minding prisoners. She says I care more about marshalin' than her. That I ain't even brung you down to see the house.'

'House ain't finished, is it?' I said.

'Nope.'

'I was figuring to come down when it was,' I said.

'Go on down and take a look at it,' Cole said. 'Calm Allie down a little. Tell her you like it.'

'It's raining like hell,' I said.

'Go ahead,' Cole said. 'I'll mind the prisoners.'

'I ain't a prisoner,' Whitfield said.

'No, a 'course you ain't,' Cole said. 'I wasn't thinkin'. I'm sorry about sayin' it.'

'Got a roof on it yet?' I said.

'Sure has,' Cole said. 'Tight one, too. I got me a carpenter used to build boats in Rhode Island.'

'Long as I don't get a soaking while I'm admiring the work,' I said.

'You go on down there,' Cole said. 'Allie's down there with an umbrella, planning the furniture.'

Cole sat at his desk with his coat and hat still on. I put on my hat and slicker and went out into the rain. I stayed on the boardwalk. The street was mud by now, probably deep above my ankles. Enough to suck the boot right off your foot. I was all right until I got to Front Street. Cole's house was on the other side, and I had to drag through the mud to get across. At the building site, I mucked a few more yards to the house and stepped up onto the first-floor decking. Allie was there, with her skirts tucked up, wearing a pair of men's boots that was much too big for her, and carrying an umbrella, still open, even under the in-place roof. Cole had been right. It didn't leak.

'Everett,' she said. 'Oh my God, look at me.'

She bent over and untucked her skirt, letting it fall over the big, wet boots.

'You look fine to me, Allie.'

'I must look like a drowned cat,' she said. 'My hair all wet, and these boots . . .'

'You always look good, Allie.'

'You're too kind, Everett.'

'House is hurrying right along,' I said.

'Yes,' Allie said. 'It's going to be very grand. If Virgil ever bothers to come live in it.'

'Pretty sure he will,' I said.

'Don't pay no attention to the house,' she said. 'Hell, Everett. He don't pay no attention to me. Just sits up there in the jail with his gun, being marshal.'

'Well,' I said. 'Been sorta lively of late.'

'It's his job,' Allie said. 'It's not his damn life.'

'Well,' I said, 'show me around. I'll tell him about it.'

She had, as we talked, moved closer to me. Now she took my hand and began to lead me around the various rooms that had been studded off.

'We'll have our parlor here,' she said, 'where we can look out and see who's coming to call. And this will be the kitchen.'

There's always something sort of dreamish about being sheltered on a rainy day. The rain drummed pleasantly on the roof. And, as it fell outside, it formed a kind of silvery curtain around the open sides of the unfinished building. There was coziness inside under the roof, even though there were no walls. Allie still held the hand with which she'd led me through the small framing. Her shoulder touched my arm.

'You think it will be nice, Everett?'

'It'll be elegant,' I said.

She rubbed her cheek against my shoulder.

'Will you come often and visit us?'

'Every time I'm invited.'

'I can cook, you know,' Allie said.

She had put her hand on my back and was beginning to move it up and down my spine.

'I never thought you couldn't,' I said.

She turned in toward me and put both arms around my waist. She looked up at me, and her eyes looked sort of dazed, as if she wasn't focusing too well.

'Do you think I'm pretty?'

'Yes.'

I sounded hoarse. I felt as if my throat had closed up a little. She tightened her arms around my waist and pressed herself against me, arching her back a little to look up at me. The movement made her pelvis press against me, and caused me some excitement.

'Allie,' I said.

'I want you to kiss me, Everett.'

'Allie,' I said again. 'I think we ought to stop here.'

She slid her hands up my back and behind my neck and pulled herself up on tiptoes and bent my head down toward her a little and kissed me hard with her mouth open. She smelled good. I kissed her back. Then I forced her away from me and held her there at arm's length.

'I'm with Virgil,' I said. 'And so are you.'

'Virgil's not here,' she said. 'Mostly, Virgil's never here.'

She was trying to press back against me.

'Ain't true, Allie,' I said. 'But even if it was, we ain't with each other. We're both with him.'

She was silent; her face had turned white. She was pressing hard against my hands as I held her away.

'Allie,' I said. 'For Christ's sake, we're right out in the open here.'

'Let me go,' she said.

Her voice was harsh and unlovely.

'Let me go, goddamn you,' she said.

'I'm leaving, Allie,' I said.

'You bastard,' she said. 'You sonova bitch.'

The words came out slurred and almost hissing with rage. Her face was perfectly white and twisted with anger. There were tears in her eyes, though she wasn't crying yet. I gave her a little shove that set her back for a moment and turned and ran.

'You prick,' she screamed after me.

I ran through the sucking mud and got up on the dry boardwalk and walked fast up Front Street toward Second.

'You fucking prick,' she screamed.

I hunched my shoulders a little and kept walking through the hard rain.

CHAPTER 22

Vince came back with twenty riders on a hot, still day with no clouds and a hard sun. I was sitting out front with Whitfield when they turned the corner at Second Street and started down toward us at a slow walk, nobody saying anything.

'God, Jesus,' Whitfield said and stood up.

'There's a loaded gun in the table drawer,' I said to him. 'If they rush us, shoot Bragg.'

Whitfield went inside the office. I took out my Colt and fired two shots in the air and reloaded and holstered. A couple of the horses in Vince's party shied at the gunfire. No one else reacted. I picked up the eight-gauge and stood. There were people on the sidewalks on Main Street. As the riders approached, the people disappeared into the nearest doors. The riders fanned out across the street behind Vince three rows deep, halted in front of the office, and turned their horses toward me. The riders in the second and third rows moved slowly sideways to form a big single-file circle in front of me. Some of them had Winchesters.

'Morning, Hitch,' Vince said to me.

'Vince,' I said.

'We come for Mr Bragg,' Vince said.

'Can't have him,' I said.

'We'll take him if we have to.'

The rider on the far right end of the circle had a riderless saddle horse on a lead. To my right, Virgil Cole came walking on the boardwalk toward us. He didn't seem to raise his voice, but everyone heard him clear.

'If you do, he'll be dead.'

No one said anything.

'Everett,' Cole said, 'you step on into the office with that eight-gauge and first thing, anything happens, you blow Mr Bragg's head off.'

I wanted to say that Whitfield had that assignment and I could do him more good out here. But I didn't. I did what he told me. I always did what he told me, because in a lot of towns over a lot of years, I'd learned that in a tight crease, you'd best do what Virgil Cole told you. No questions. Virgil always knew the situation better than you did, and he always knew what he was doing better than anyone did. I reached behind me and pushed open the office door and went inside.

Behind me, I heard Cole say, 'You boys best wheel them animals around and shoo.'

I glanced over my shoulder at Bragg.

Bragg was standing in his cell, close to the bars, looking at me.

'We come for Bragg,' Vince said.

96

I glanced at Whitfield. There was no Whitfield. Past the two cells was a door that led down a little hall to the store behind us that sold dry goods and hardware. The door was open.

'Can't have him,' Cole said.

I went and closed it and slid the bolt. Bragg smiled at me.

'We know you're good, Cole,' I heard Vince say. 'But you ain't as good as twenty of us.'

'You know the arrangement, boys,' Cole said pleasantly.

I went to the table drawer and opened it. The gun Whitfield was supposed to use was still there.

'First time one of you does an ineluctable thing . . .' Cole said.

He didn't finish the sentence. But I knew, because I'd seen him do this before, that he had pointed at the office and pretended to shoot Bragg with his thumb and forefinger.

'You can't just shoot a prisoner,' Vince said. 'You're a fucking lawman.'

I smiled. Cole already had them backing up a little. He didn't need me out there with the shotgun.

It ain't firepower, he'd always said. *It was firepower, we'd lose most of the time, because most of the time it's just you and me against a whole passel.*

'Prisoner tries to escape, I'm supposed to shoot him,' Cole said.

'You shoot him, you think we'll ride off?'

'Nope.'

'We'll kill you and Hitch,' Vince said.

'You'll try.'

'There's twenty of us, for God's sake,' Vince said. 'You willing to die to keep us from taking him?'

'Sure,' Cole said.

Everyone was silent. I could see Vince staring hard at Cole. Vince was a hard case. Jack Bell had been a hard case. But Vince was looking at something Vince had never seen before.

'Hitch?' Vince raised his voice. 'You willing to die, too?'

I stood near the corner of the two cells, against the wall, where I wouldn't get shot right away, and where I could get a clear shot at Bragg if they came. I could see Vince and some of the riders through the window. I couldn't see Cole.

''Course he's willin' to die,' Cole said. 'You think we do this kinda work 'cause we scared to die?'

Even though I couldn't see him, I knew how he was. I'd seen him at other times. He was motionless. His six-gun was still holstered. His arms were relaxed at his side. He was looking at Vince with no expression, and his eyes were perfectly dead, like two stones.

'Any man's scared a dying,' Vince said.

'He's got 'em turned,' I said softly to Bragg. 'They're arguing with him.'

Bragg was silent, struggling, I assumed, with hope, fear, and rage.

'You?' Cole said.

Vince said, 'Me?'

'You afraid to die,' Cole said.

'I ain't afraid,' he said.

'Good,' Cole said. ''Cause you go first.'

Vince rocked very slightly back in his saddle. He probably didn't know that he'd done it.

'Ball goes up,' Cole said. 'Two things certain. Bragg's dead. You're dead.'

Then I could see Cole. He had stepped forward to the edge of the boardwalk so he was closer to Vince. He appeared to be looking straight at him, but he pointed, apparently without looking, off to his right.

'And the boy with the Winchester,' Cole said, 'with the red scarf. He goes next.'

The way Cole could see all around him was always sort of magical. And I knew he meant it. I'd been with him in so many gunfights that I knew what he'd do. If it started, he'd shoot Vince long before Vince got a hand on his weapon; then, if there was someone with a rifle, he'd wheel in a comfortable crouch and shoot him. Then, when he'd emptied the sidearm, if he was still alive, he'd dive through the open office door and continue matters with the Winchester he kept just inside. As soon as I'd killed Bragg, of course, I would be shooting past him through the window. No one said anything for a long, quiet moment. Then Cole stepped off the boardwalk and into the street.

'Go on home, Vince,' Cole said. 'Too many people die if you don't.'

He took his hat off with his left hand and swatted

Vince's horse across the face. The horse reared and wheeled half around. Cole slapped it on the hindquarters, and the horse reared against the bit and tried to run, with Vince wrestling hard to hold him.

'Go on,' Cole said, pushing among the horses, his right hand hanging loose near his gun, his left hand slapping with the hat. 'Go on home.'

It's always one person at a time, Cole would tell me. *No matter how many there are, you back them down one at a time so it's always you against him. And he knows you're quicker.*

Vince brought his surging horse under control and held him.

'There'll be another time, Cole,' he said.

Then he gave the horse his head, and one after the other, Bragg's riders headed out of town.

CHAPTER 23

As soon as the riders were gone, I came out of the office, still carrying the eight-gauge. I took each barrel off cock as I came.

'Whitfield run off,' I said.

'Too bad,' Cole said.

He had his hat back on and set right, and as far as you could tell, he had just gotten up from a nap.

Up the street, Allie French came out of the Boston House and ran along the boardwalk toward Cole.

'Oh, Virgil,' she said. 'Virgil.'

Cole stood and waited.

'Oh, Virgil,' she said again. 'Are you all right?'

'I am,' Cole said.

She ran right into him and pressed her face against his chest and put her arms around him.

'That was the bravest thing I've ever seen. Just you and all those men. That was wonderful.'

Cole seemed a little uneasy about what to do. Being Virgil Cole, he didn't show much. But he stood still with his arms at his sides and didn't look at anything.

'Everett was with me,' he said.

People had come out of the shops and saloons and housing, where they had earlier taken refuge.

'Oh, pooh on Everett,' Allie said. 'He was inside, hiding. It was you out there all alone, Virgil. That was heroic.'

'Everett wasn't exactly hiding, Allie.'

The people began to gather round, looking at Cole and Allie. I saw Katie Goode in the crowd and nodded at her. Allie lifted her face from Cole's chest and turned toward the crowd, her arms still holding on to Cole in proud ownership.

'Isn't that the most heroic thing you folks have ever seen?' she said.

Somebody began to clap, and then pretty soon everyone was clapping. Allie stood, holding on to Cole, smiling at the crowd as if they were clapping for her. I was watching Cole. For maybe the first time since I'd met him, he didn't quite know what was going on. And he didn't quite know what to do about it.

'That'll be fine,' he said to the crowd. 'That'll be fine.'

Then he turned away and steered Allie away, and they walked into the marshal's office.

As they went by, Cole said softly to me, 'Send them home, Everett.'

After I got the crowd moving, I walked with Katie Goode back toward the Boston House.

'You need a drink?' she said.

'Be nice,' I said.

'Yesterday was payday at the mine,' Katie said. 'I'll buy.'

'Be nice,' I said.

We had a table near the bar. I drank some beer. Katie had a whiskey.

'Mr Raines don't normally want us to drink in here,' Katie said. 'But if I'm with you, he won't say nothing.'

'So you had more reason than just how good-lookin' I am,' I said. 'To buy me a beer.'

'Good-lookin's enough,' she said.

Some miners who still had money left were lining the bar. The rainstorm had broken the heat, and it was cool again today, with some air moving in through the street door.

'He really is something,' Katie said. 'Isn't he?'

She had on a flowered dress with puffy shoulders and a bonnet. She could have been a ranch woman, or a miner's wife, except she looked too good, and she smelled sort of soapy. She told me once that she washed herself all over, every day.

'Virgil?' I said. 'I ain't seen a man like Virgil Cole, ever.'

'Is he really not afraid to die?'

'Never seen no sign of it,' I said.

'Does he feel anything?'

'I don't know. I believe he's feeling something for Allie French.'

'Her,' Katie said.

'Don't know how many women Virgil's ever actually spent time with. I mean, he has women whenever he wants them, but it's mostly in and out real quick, without much conversation.'

'Lotta men are like that,' Katie said.

'Yes,' I said. 'I imagine. But I ain't sure Virgil ever had a woman call him heroic, 'cept she was drunk and had her drawers off.'

'Did you like her little performance?' Katie said.

'Not so much,' I said.

'You think Mr Cole liked it?'

'Hard to say what Virgil likes,' I said. 'He wasn't Virgil Cole, I'd say he might have been embarrassed.'

'Or flattered.'

'Yeah, maybe,' I said. 'Virgil don't normally think about things like that.'

'That's an evil woman, Everett.'

I didn't say anything.

'She is,' Katie said. 'I know about evil women, Everett, and I know about sex. And I know how silly men are about it.'

'Not all of us,' I said.

'No, you seem pretty level, Everett. I got to say that. But I'll bet you when Mr Cole's not around, she flirts with you.'

'How do you know that?' I said.

'She does,' Katie said. 'Don't she?'

'Yes,' I said. 'Fact is, she got kind of hot with me when we were looking at the new house Virgil's building for her.'

Katie smiled, as if she was wise. Which she wasn't really. But she had Allie's number.

'What did you do?' Katie said.

'I run off,' I said.

'You say anything to Mr Cole.'

'No.'

'You going to say anything?'

'No. Virgil couldn't hear something like that.'

She sipped a little of her whiskey, watching me over the rim of the glass.

'And I don't want him knowing anything about it from you. I ain't told anybody else, so if he finds out, I'll know who couldn't keep her mouth closed.'

'I won't tell,' Katie said. 'But ain't it so, Everett, sometimes I been with you, you didn't want me keeping my mouth closed.'

She looked straight at me and we both laughed.

'There'll be those times again,' I said.

'Surely,' Katie said, and sipped whiskey. 'But you're his friend, Everett. Don't you think you ought to tell him?'

'Can't,' I said. 'He couldn't hear it.'

'What if she tells him?'

'Why would she tell him?' I said.

'I tole you, she's evil,' Katie said. 'What if she tells him and says it was your doing.'

'He'll kill me,' I said.

Katie frowned and looked down at her whiskey glass, studying the brown surface of the whiskey.

'Sooner, or later,' Katie said, 'she's gonna tell him.'

CHAPTER 24

The next morning Whitfield came into the marshal's office looking bad.

'I slept in the feed loft,' he said, 'at the livery stable.'

'Well,' Cole said, 'you come back.'

'I can't face up to guns no more,' Whitfield said.

'But you'll testify,' Cole said.

'I will.'

'That's fine,' Cole said. 'Everett and me will face up to the guns.'

Bragg, leaning against the bars of his cell, said, 'You gonna get your chance, too, Whitfield.'

It was like I could see the skin tighten on Whitfield's face, and the fear come in. Cole took his feet off the tabletop and stood and walked over to the cell. He stood close to the bars, an inch or so away from Bragg.

'We been treating you kindly,' Cole said to Bragg. 'In return for that, we expect you to speak when spoken to and otherwise stay quiet.'

'I can talk if I want to,' Bragg said.

'And me and Everett can come into that cell and lock the door behind us and beat the sweet

Jesus hell right out of you every morning instead of breakfast.'

'You wouldn't talk that way if I had a gun,' Bragg said.

'Don't matter if I would or wouldn't,' Cole said, 'fact is you don't, and I do, so the point appears mute.'

Bragg met Cole's look for a bit and then couldn't hold it, and turned away and sat on his bunk. Cole walked back and sat at his desk and put his feet up.

'Don't pay him too much mind,' he said to Whitfield.

'He's right, though,' Whitfield said. 'What about after the trial?'

'After the trial, Bragg goes to prison, and Everett and me escort you to a faraway place of your choosing,' Cole said.

'And before the trial.'

'You stay right here with us,' Cole said.

'And him,' Whitfield said, and nodded at Bragg.

'He ain't pleasant,' Cole said. 'But he can't do you no harm.'

'What if his men come back?'

'They won't come back,' Cole said.

People believed Cole when he talked. He was always clear on what he knew. He never claimed anything he didn't know, and he always meant what he said.

'Could I maybe stay in the hotel?'

Cole shook his head.

'That splits us up,' he said. 'Means one of us got to go with you and the other one got to stay here with Bragg.'

'But if they won't come back?'

'Maybe somebody else,' Cole said.

'You think they'll send somebody?'

'Don't matter what I think. You ever hear of this fella Clausewitz?'

'Who?'

'Clausewitz, German fella, wrote a book about war. This Clausewitz says you got to prepare for what your enemy *can* do, not what you think he *might* do.'

'Clausewitz?'

'What I'm saying is splitting our forces ain't to our advantage.'

'You been reading Clausewitz on war?' I said.

'Certainly. You ever read it?'

'I read it at West Point,' I said.

'Good book,' Cole said.

I nodded. Whitfield looked lost.

'Virgil,' I said, 'you are a surprising man.'

CHAPTER 25

Judge Elias Callison came to town on an early-evening train with his law clerk and four sheriff's deputies. And after they got settled into the Boston House, the law clerk, whose name was Eaton, and the lead deputy, fella named Stringer, came down to the marshal's office to talk with Cole. Stringer had a deputy's star on his shirt and wore a long-barreled Colt butt-forward on the left.

'That him?' Stringer said.

'That's Bragg,' Cole said.

Stringer went to the cell and looked in.

'Tall,' Stringer said.

'Fella in the other cell is Whitfield, the witness.'

'How come he's in jail?'

'Fears for his life,' Cole said. 'So me 'n Everett here are lookin' after him until we finish with Bragg.'

Stringer nodded slowly. He was a tall, thin man with a big moustache and the sort of leatherish look of a man who had spent a lot of time in the saddle. Whitfield's cell door was ajar, and Whitfield was sitting on his bunk, reading his Bible, his lips moving slowly as he puzzled it out. Stringer left Bragg and looked in at him.

'You gonna testify?' Stringer asked.

'Yes, sir.'

'If he don't die a' fright first,' Bragg said from his cell.

'I'll testify,' Whitfield said.

Stringer nodded.

'I know you will,' he said.

'Bragg got a lawyer?' Eaton asked.

'Nope.'

'He needs a lawyer,' Eaton said.

He was short and plump with a round face. He didn't look like he rode horses much.

'Surely does,' Cole said.

'No, I mean we ain't going to just ride over here and convict him,' Eaton said. 'Judge Callison's a real bear on the law. Got to be a fair trial. He's got to have a lawyer, and there's got to be evidence.'

Cole stared at him as if he'd never heard such a thing in his life, which wasn't true. He probably knew more about trials than Eaton did.

'Hear that, Bragg,' Cole said. 'You gotta get you a lawyer.'

'I don't know no lawyers,' Bragg said.

'There's a justice of the peace,' I said. 'Name of Mueller. Over in Little Springs. I can ride over there, see if he'll do it.'

'I ain't paying no damn lawyer to help you hang me,' Bragg said.

'What do we do about that?' I said to Eaton.

'County'll pay for it,' Eaton said.

'I ain't talking to no fucking lawyer,' Bragg said.

'Doesn't matter, Mr Bragg,' Eaton said. 'County'll give you one. Up to you if you talk or listen.'

'Whyn't you ride on over there,' Cole said to me.

'We'll help with Bragg and Whitfield,' Stringer said. 'Sooner that JP gets here, the sooner we have the trial. And the sooner I take him down to Yaqui Prison and watch him hanged.'

'You know what he done,' Cole said.

Stringer nodded.

'I know what he done.'

CHAPTER 26

I brought Mueller back from Little Springs, and Judge Callison set a trial date in one week, so counsel could prepare a defense. The judge also ordered the deputies to take charge of the prisoner until then. Since there wasn't no place to take charge of him except where he was, the deputies sort of moved into the marshal's office, so Cole and me spent more of our time sitting around in the Boston House in the saloon, or watching them doing the finish work on Cole's house.

We were drinking coffee in the saloon one morning when I saw Cole sit up a little straighter and drop one hand lightly into his lap near his gun's butt. I looked where he was looking and saw two men who looked like each other leaning on the bar. One of them nodded at Cole. He nodded back. The other one grinned.

'You know them?' I said.

'Shelton brothers,' Cole said.

'Can't say I know them.'

''Fore you was doing this work,' Cole said.

'They troublesome?' I said.

'Yes.'

'They ain't packing,' I said. 'That I can see.'

'You'll know when they're packing,' Cole said.

'Good?'

'Excellent,' Cole said.

'Good as you and me?'

'Might be,' Cole said. 'Don't know that they ain't.'

'One of 'em shoot better than the other?'

'Can't say. Ring's the older brother, on the right. Other one's name is Mackie.'

'Do look alike,' I said.

'They are alike. And they're close. Never seen nobody closer. See one, you see 'em both.'

'Fight one?' I said.

Cole nodded.

'Fight 'em both,' he said.

'They do law work?' I said.

'They do gun work,' Cole said.

'So what would they be doing here?'

'Might have something to do with Bragg.'

I looked at the Shelton brothers for a while. Ring had taken his hat off when he had come in, and set it on the bar. He didn't have much hair, except for a kind of long fringe that looked like it was turning gray. He had a thick neck and longish arms and sloping shoulders that looked strong but not all that wide. His legs were bowed some, and it made him shorter than he might have been otherwise. Mackie had his hat still on. He was taller than Ring, and his legs were straighter. The hair that showed under his hat was sort of reddish. But he had the same thick neck and long arms. There was a bottle of whiskey on the bar between them, and each of them had a glass. Ring picked up the bottle, and he and Mackie came to the table.

'Virgil,' Ring said.

'Ring.'

'You remember my brother,' Ring said.

Virgil nodded.

'Mackie.'

Mackie said, 'Virgil.'

'This here is Everett Hitch,' Virgil said.

We all nodded.

'Can we set?' Ring said.

Virgil gestured toward the empty chairs. Ring put the whiskey bottle on the table, and the Shelton brothers sat down.

'Want a taste?' Ring said.

Virgil shook his head and tapped the marshal star on his shirt.

'Still doin' that,' Ring said.

Virgil nodded.

'Well, we ain't,' Ring said.

He poured some whiskey into Mackie's glass and some into his own. He sipped some of his and smiled.

'Good,' he said. 'Think it's corn.'

He looked at me.

'You as good as Virgil with a gun?' he said.

'Never been tested,' I said.

'I hear you been with him for a while.'

'I have.'

'So you seen him work; what would you guess, you and him was to go at it?'

'Never seen no one better than Virgil,' I said.

'But you ain't saying you're not as good.'

'I ain't discussing it, the truth be told,' I said. 'How 'bout you?'

'Like you,' Ring said. 'Never seen no one better.'

'You ever meet anybody better'n you, Virgil?'

'Guess I haven't,' Cole said. 'I'm still here.'

'Guess that's true,' Ring said. 'How 'bout him?' He nodded at me.

'He'll do,' Cole said.

'He as good as us?' Ring said. 'Me and Mackie?'

'He'll do,' Cole said.

I was looking at Ring's hands. With his thick shoulders and his bowed legs, Ring looked like a cowboy. But his hands on the tabletop were clean and flexible, and the nails were trimmed. I thought they looked like the kind of hands you might see on a painter.

'What are you and Mackie doing in town?' Cole said.

'Everybody got to be somewhere, don't they, Mackie?'

Mackie nodded. Where his brother had sort of wide eyes that bulged a little, Mackie's looked heavy-lidded and half open all the time.

'Gonna be here long?' Cole said.

'Can't say. Heard there was a big trial comin' up, might want to take that in. I like a good trial,' Ring said. 'Mackie, too.'

'Well,' Cole said. 'You been in some of my towns before. You know the rules.'

'I surely do,' Ring said. 'You know the rules, don't you, Mackie?'

Mackie had a mouthful of whiskey. He swallowed.

'I know them rules,' he said.

His voice was a kind of hoarse whisper. It sounded as if it was an effort to speak. Across the room, Allie French came in wearing a pink dress and came straight up behind Cole and kissed him on the top of his head, and stood with her arms draped over his shoulders.

'This here is Mrs French,' Cole said.

They all said hello. Ring and Mackie both looked at her steadily. She looked back at them without flinching. The king's lady. Let them stare. Cole didn't like it much. But he hadn't made any laws about looking at Allie French. He stood.

'Mrs French and me are going perambuling in a buggy,' he said.

He put his hand on Allie's arm and turned her, and they walked out of the saloon through the lobby door. As they left, she glanced back over her shoulder at our table.

'Virgil's woman,' Ring said to me.

'Yep.'

'I'll be damned,' Ring said.

'Is sort of surprising,' I said.

'I always figure Virgil for whores and squaws.'

'She's neither one of them,' I said.

'I'll be damned.'

'You known Virgil for a time?' I said.

'Oh, hell, yes, me, and then when Mackie got old enough, me and Mackie both. Knew him in Wichita. Was with him in Lincoln County. Did some business with him in Bisbee. Up along the Platte.'

'Deputy work?'

'Some.'

'Not deputy work?'

Ring grinned. I noticed he had a couple of teeth gone in front.

'Some,' he said.

He and Mackie both drank some more whiskey. It didn't seem to affect them.

'After the trial, you gonna hang this fella here?' Ring said.

'Ain't mine to say.'

'No, course not,' Ring said. 'I hope it's here. Me and Mackie like hangings. Still there ain't no gallows, and nobody building one. It's messy if you hang 'em from a rafter or something.'

I nodded. I knew that if he was convicted, they'd take Bragg to Yaqui and hang him in the prison courtyard. But I didn't see any reason to tell the Sheltons. Keeping quiet never caused me no trouble. I stood.

'Nice meetin' you boys,' I said.

'Likewise,' Ring said.

Mackie nodded. None of us offered to shake hands. There was no advantage to letting somebody get hold of you.

CHAPTER 27

It was the night before the trial. Stringer and his deputies were in the jail with Bragg and Whitfield. Cole and I were walking, one on each side of Allie, to look at the latest developments on the house. Allie had her arm though Cole's. She showed no sign that anything had gone on there, or anywhere else, between me and her.

'Tell me about those men, Virgil,' she said.

'Shelton brothers?'

'Yes. The ones in the Boston House Saloon.'

'They're just gunmen,' Cole said.

'But they seem different than other gunmen.'

'They ain't,' Cole said. 'They're just real good gunmen.'

'No,' she said, 'they are different. Even from Mr Bragg. You treat them different.'

'Known 'em a long time,' Cole said.

'Longer than you've known Everett.'

'Yep.'

'Have you and they been friends?'

'Ain't been enemies.'

'But you don't act like they're friends now.'

'Never were friends,' Cole said. 'Done some work with them.'

'Shooting work?'

'Yep.'

'Can they shoot as good as you?'

'Ain't never been put to the test,' Cole said.

'I never seen anyone, Allie,' I said, 'good as Virgil with a gun.'

'Maybe so, maybe not,' Cole said. 'Ain't but one way to know. And knowing ain't the point.'

'I know, Virgil, I was just trying to answer Allie's question.'

'Ain't no answer. Ain't a question to ask,' Cole said. 'Ain't like we're racing horses.'

Allie was watching us both, her eyes shifting back and forth between us. She seemed sort of excited. Her eyes were shiny.

'Don't be careless with them boys, Everett,' Cole said. 'They are quick and they hit what they shoot at.'

'One of them more than the other?' I said.

'No.'

'What happened to the younger one's voice?' Allie said.

'Took a bullet in the throat,' Cole said. 'Up in Cheyenne, I believe.'

'Are they going to cause trouble?' Allie said.

Her eyes were even shinier. Her face looked sort of hot. There was a reddish smudge over her cheekbones.

'Might,' Cole said. 'Often do.'

'Are you afraid of them?' Allie said.

Her voice sounded a bit scratchy, like she might need to clear her throat. Cole listened to the question and was quiet like he always was when he was thinking about a question. He turned it around in his head, looked at it from all its various sides, and decided.

'No,' he said. 'I ain't.'

CHAPTER 28

Cole and I were sitting outside the office with the door open so we could hear if Bragg tried to gnaw through the bars. It was a warm day with no clouds and a bright sun.

'You and Allie going to get married?' I said.

'If she'll have me,' Cole said.

'I figure you and her building that house together,' I said, 'means something.'

Cole nodded.

'Anything happens to me, Everett,' he said, 'I'd appreciate you lookin' out for her.'

'You expecting anything special?' I said.

'This is uncertain kind of work we do,' Cole said.

'Yes, it is.'

'Allie's better if she's with someone,' Cole said.

'She needs help,' I said, 'I'll help her.'

'She's not good bein' alone,' Cole said.

I nodded. A hawk was circling low over the town, looking for rats maybe, or mice, or ground squirrels, or whatever it could find out back of Café Paris.

'She seems like a pretty strong woman to me, Virgil.'

'She's stronger with a man,' Cole said.

No matter how much time I'd spent with Cole, he still surprised me. He appeared to understand Allie a lot better than I would have said he could. We both watched the hawk for a time as it wheeled on the low wind currents.

'Shelton brothers bothering you?' I said.

'I'm thinking about 'em,' Cole said.

'You figure they are here because of Bragg?'

'Seems sort of coinciding,' Cole said, 'them boys should drift in here just before Bragg's trial.'

'You think they got hired to bust him out?'

'Might've.'

'Or kill Whitfield? They kill Whitfield, there's no need to bust Bragg out, because we can't convict him.'

'Deputies took Whitfield over to Fort Beale,' Cole said. 'They'll keep him there till the trial.'

'Who's idea was that?'

'Mine.'

'So you did think maybe they was here to kill Whitfield,' I said.

'Couldn't say they wasn't.'

'Who's going to bring him in to testify?'

'Stringer and the other deputies.'

'Sheltons know where Whitfield is?'

'Nobody does, except me, and now you.'

'He testifies, and they'll convict Bragg,' I said.

'I'd say so.'

'So if the Sheltons are here about Bragg,' I said, 'they got to bust him out afterwards.'

'Yep.'

''Course, they may not be here for that,' I said.

'Nope.'

'On the other hand, there's Mr Clausewitz.'

'Yep.'

'So we got to prepare for it.'

Cole nodded.

'We got you and me and four deputies, Virgil,' I said. 'Sounds like enough to me.'

Cole tilted his head back against the top of the chair as if he was looking at the sky, except his eyes were closed. He sat like that for a pretty long time.

Then he said, 'Four deputies won't count for much if it happens.'

'They look like pretty good gun hands,' I said. ''Specially Stringer.'

'They are pretty good gun hands,' Cole said.

'But not good enough?'

'Everett,' Cole said. 'Neither you or me ain't never been up against nobody like Ring and Mackie Shelton.'

We were both quiet as the hawk swooped and soared on the wind.

'We been up against pretty good,' I said.

Cole shook his head without remark.

'You ain't sure we can beat them,' I said after a while.

'When it comes right down to her,' Cole said. 'No, I ain't.'

I thought about it.

'Well,' I said after a time. 'It's not like you ever know for sure, before the shooting starts.'

'So this time won't be much different,' Cole said.

'Be different if we lose,' I said.

'Won't matter to us,' Cole said. ''Cept for Allie.'

CHAPTER 29

Whitfield testified, with the bar closed in the Boston House Saloon, and Cole beside him, and me in a lookout chair with a shotgun, and two country deputies with Winchesters at the saloon doors. He stood up, and Eaton swore him in, and the judge asked him what he seen when Jack Bell was shot, and Whitfield looked right at Bragg and said Bragg done it. The tables had been pushed to the walls for the trial, and the chairs had been set up in rows. Most of the town was there. The Sheltons sat near the lobby door, in the back.

There was no prosecutor. The judge asked Whitfield questions, and then Mueller, Bragg's lawyer, cross-examined. You could see his heart wasn't in it. He knew Bragg was guilty, and he knew that Judge Callison knew it. Whitfield was the only witness against Bragg. Mueller called Bragg's foreman. Vince said he didn't see who shot Bell and the deputy, but it wasn't Bragg. Mueller brought three more of Bragg's hands to the stand. They all said the same thing. When Mueller brought the fourth, the judge stopped him.

'You gonna say anything different?' the judge said to the hand.

'Nope.'

The judge addressed the room.

'Anybody in the court got anything different to say other than Bragg didn't shoot anyone and you don't know who did?'

No one stirred. Judge Callison nodded to himself.

'That'll do then; no reason to waste time saying the same thing over and over.'

'My client has a right to testify in his own defense,' Mueller said.

''Course he does,' the judge said. 'Swear him in, Eaton.'

Eaton took the Bible to Bragg. Bragg looked at it without comment.

'Put your hand on the Bible,' Eaton said.

Bragg didn't move. Cole reached over and picked up one of Bragg's hands and slapped it onto the Bible, and held it in place. Bragg didn't resist. Eaton said the words. Bragg didn't answer.

'He so swears,' Judge Callison said. 'What have you got to say for yourself, Mr Bragg.'

Bragg stood slowly.

'Fred Whitfield is a goddamned liar. I didn't shoot Jack Bell or them other fellas. I don't know what happened to them.'

He sat down. Judge Callison looked at him for a moment and half smiled.

'Eloquent, Mr Bragg. But unconvincing,' he said. 'I find you guilty of these charges and sentence

127

you to hang at Yaqui Prison at a time to be decided by the prison warden.'

He banged his gavel and said, 'Court's adjourned.'

And that was Bragg's trial. Stringer and Cole and I and the other deputies took him back to his cell.

CHAPTER 30

There was no one at the train siding in Appaloosa. The westbound train to Yaqui was twenty minutes late, and by the time we got Bragg, in handcuffs and leg shackles, onto the train and into the last passenger car, it was 6:20 in the morning. Cole sat beside him, and I sat across the aisle with Stringer and his three deputies in front of us. All of us were yawning. I had a shotgun; everyone else had Winchesters. All of us carried sidearms. There was no one else in the car except a couple of drummers up front, both of whom were asleep.

The conductor came through. Stringer gave him a county voucher for all of us.

'Be about seven hours to Yaqui,' the conductor said. 'Be stopping for water at Chester.'

Cole nodded.

Stringer said, 'I know. I've done this before.'

The conductor looked at Bragg.

'He ain't going to be no trouble, is he?' the conductor said.

'If he is, it won't be for long,' Cole said.

Bragg stared out the window as the train slowly

129

began to move, and he kept looking as we picked up speed. I had not heard him say anything since the trial. Cole ignored him.

'Anything gonna happen,' Cole said to me, 'it'll be at Chester. Takes 'em a while to fill that boiler, and we're pretty much sitting ducks while they do.'

'That why we're along?' I said. 'Because you think something might happen.'

'Yep. Usually, I'd just let them boys take him over to Yaqui.'

'You think it'll be the Sheltons?'

'Yep.'

I looked at the four deputies.

'These are four pretty good boys, Virgil.'

'They are,' Virgil said.

The train moved heavily along the tracks that ran beside the river, across Bragg's ranch. We could see the ranch house and some of the outbuildings off to the right side of the train. I thought for a minute what it might be like to sit in shackles on your way to hang and look out at your home and not be able to go there. I decided there was nothing to be gained thinking about that, so I stopped. A few of Bragg's steers stood near the tracks, staring at us as we went by.

We stayed in the flatlands pretty much, following the course of the river, the tracks snaking along around the hills. Out the left side, at a distance, I could see the Appaloosa stallion herding his mares toward a draw. The sun was higher now, and the train was getting warm. One of the deputies opened

130

the windows that would open and let the air move in as we chugged along. A couple of antelope stood on one of the hills above us as we went west, and on another hill, among the rock outcroppings, six or eight coyotes sat staring down at us, and we bumped and rattled past them. One of the train hands came through after a while and gave us coffee. Bragg, too. All of us took it.

'Be some sandwiches at Chester,' the train hand said.

'How soon?' one of the deputies said.

'Chester? Hell,' he said. 'I dunno, ask the conductor.'

The deputy nodded as if he'd expected the answer. A half hour later, the conductor strolled through and took out a big watch and studied it for a minute and told us we'd be in Chester in one hour and thirty-six minutes.

'When we start the upgrade,' the conductor said, 'you'll feel us slow down. It ain't a hell of a grade, but it's a long one, and the locomotive labors a little.'

'How long after we hit the grade?' Cole said.

'Ten minutes or so, ain't far, but the engine's strugglin'.'

'Anybody there.'

'Nope.'

'Thanks,' Cole said.

I looked at Bragg. He was still staring out the window without expression. If he expected action at Chester, he wasn't letting on.

'When we get there,' Cole said to me, 'I'll go to the front of the car. You take the rear. Outside. I don't want us sitting in here like a tom at a turkey shoot.'

'Sure,' I said.

Cole was the first to sense the start of the upgrade. Of course. He always knew things first. I hadn't felt the train slow at all, when Cole was on his feet.

'You boys stay here with the prisoner,' he said to Stringer. 'Me 'n Everett will do some recognicence.'

He picked up his Winchester, pointed me toward the back of the train, and walked toward the front. As I walked toward the rear coupling space between my car and the caboose, I could feel the train beginning to lurch up the grade. Virgil disappeared out onto the front. The strong-smelling smoke from the engine streamed back over the train. I held the handrail and swung out and looked ahead. At the top of the rise, I could see the water tower and beside it, higher, the windmill that kept it full. I could also see Virgil's head as he looked out past the cars in front of us. I scanned the dry scrubland around us. There was nothing moving. The train wasn't moving fast enough to generate any breeze, and the thick air was oppressive. I turned and looked on the other side of the train. Nothing moved over there, either. There was nothing behind us.

132

As we went over a small bridge over a shallow dry wash, three riders trailing a saddled, riderless horse on a lead appeared beside the train tracks up ahead. Two of them were the Sheltons; the other, riding between them, was Allie. Ring held the lead from the riderless horse. They rode slowly beside the train letting our car draw even with them. There was a rope around Allie's neck. The other end was looped around Ring's saddlehorn. On the other side of her, Mackie held a double-barreled shotgun resting on her shoulder, pressed against her neck. Everything slowed down. I could see the locomotive top the rise and level out as it approached the water tower. The train slowed, then halted, with the water spout over the boiler cap. I saw Cole step down from the train and stand stock-still, holding the Winchester, barrel down, in his left hand, looking at the three riders. I realized that I had stepped down, too, still holding the shotgun. There was no movement in the well shack next to the water tower, only the slow revolution of the windmill above it.

The three riders halted in front of Cole. He was motionless. So was I. The fireman had climbed onto the top of the cab to set the spout. He pulled the rope to drop it and stepped back as the water poured in, sending a slash of steam up. When he saw us all, he stopped and stared and stayed put. There was no sound but that of steam hissing from the idle engine.

'You see how this is going to go, Virgil,' Ring Shelton said.

Cole looked at the three riders without any sign. Between the two Shelton brothers Allie looked red-eyed and pale. Her face seemed crumpled.

'Any sign of trouble from anybody,' Ring said, 'and Mackie gives her both barrels. The horses will then head off in different directions, and what's left of her will be yanked off of hers, and her neck will break and she'll drag for miles through the mesquite. Less Mackie blows her head clean off, then the rope'll probably slip loose.'

He talked slowly and carefully, as if to be sure everyone understood what was being said. I didn't move. Cole looked at the three riders, unblinking. Stringer had moved out of the car and stood above the coupling behind Cole. He had his Winchester leveled at Ring. Mackie's horse swished his tail at a fly that buzzed his flank. He shifted slightly when he did, but Mackie adjusted and the shotgun stayed easy and straight against Allie's neck.

'So you folks are going to have to unshackle Bragg and parade him on out here, or she gets killed.'

Stringer had brought the Winchester to his shoulder.

'I got you in my sights,' he said. 'Whatever happens to her, you're dead.'

Ring smiled gently.

'What do you think, Virgil?' Ring said. 'Think I'll get scared and change my mind?'

134

'Put the rifle down,' Cole said to Stringer.

'This ain't your jurisdiction, Cole,' Stringer said.

'Put it down,' Cole said.

Stringer held still. Two of his deputies were on the platform behind me with Winchesters.

'I'll kill anybody don't lower the rifles,' Cole said.

It was like a painting, everyone frozen in color and time with the rolling, hardscrabble land stretching out to the horizon.

Then Stringer lowered his Winchester.

'Lower 'em, boys,' he said.

And the two deputies dropped the rifle barrels toward the ground.

'We give you Bragg, you give us the woman,' Cole said.

Ring laughed.

'Virgil, you know I ain't that dumb. You give us Bragg. We keep the woman. You ride off on the train, and when it's out of sight, we cut her loose.'

The few passengers in the other cars had gathered on our side of the train and were looking out the windows. Cole ignored them. His whole focus was on Allie and the Sheltons. He stood as he had since he'd stepped down from the train. He had not moved. He didn't move now.

Then he said, 'Everett, get Bragg.'

I looked at Stringer.

'It'll go easier with the other deputy,' I said, 'if you do it.'

Stringer held my look for a minute. Then he nodded and turned and walked back into the train.

In the silence I thought I could hear Allie sniveling. Neither of the Shelton brothers paid any attention to her except for the steady pressure of the shotgun against her neck. Then Stringer came out with Bragg. He had taken off the handcuffs and the leg shackles. Bragg stepped past him when he reached the door, and jumped down from the train and walked to the riderless horse, and swung into the saddle.

'Gimme a gun,' he said to Ring.

'Why?'

'Cole,' Bragg said. 'I'm going to shoot the sonova bitch.'

If Cole heard him, he made no sign. His gaze remained steady on the riders.

'Ain't part of the deal,' Ring said, and began to turn his horse slowly.

'Turn with us, Darlin',' he said to Allie.

'Goddammit, you work for me, gimme a fucking gun,' Bragg said.

'I hired on to get you loose,' Ring said. 'You're loose. You keep yappin' and I'll leave you and the girl right here.'

Bragg opened his mouth and closed it. He glanced down at Cole.

'Another time,' he said.

Cole didn't move.

'We'll ride off now,' Ring said. 'No hurry. We can see a long way, so best you get the train rolling, because we ain't cutting her loose until the train is out of sight, and that's a ways down the track.'

With the rope around Allie's neck tied to Ring's saddle, and Mackie on the other side with the shotgun against her neck, the three of them had to wheel in formation. Which they did slowly.

'Bragg, you lead on out,' Ring said.

Bragg glanced back at us as he rode away. Allie didn't, nor did the Sheltons.

CHAPTER 31

It took the train more than a half hour to get around the far bend and stop and back up. Cole stood on the back platform of it and said nothing as he watched the riders move away south down the dry wash. He stayed where he was and said nothing for the full half hour after the riders were no longer in sight and the train had gone around the bend and stopped and backed slowly up. When we got back to the water tower, Allie wasn't there. Virgil stepped off the train and walked toward the wash. Stringer started to walk after him.

'Stay away from him,' I said.

'The bastards said they'd leave her here.'

'They're safer if they got her,' I said.

'You knew they were lying.'

'We both knew,' I said. 'But there wasn't nothing to be done about it.'

'We got to discuss this,' Stringer said.

'Discuss it with me,' I said. 'Don't try to talk to Virgil.'

Stringer stared after Virgil.

'We got no horses,' Stringer said. 'We can't go after them on foot.'

I nodded.

'We'll go back to town and get some,' I said.

'Quicker Cole gets back here,' Stringer said, 'quicker we're on our way.'

'He won't come back,' I said.

'Won't come back?'

I shook my head.

'Wait for me,' I said and walked after Cole.

Cole was standing on the little bridge over the wash, looking south down the wash.

I said, 'We got no horses, Virgil.'

A half mile or so away, the wash curved slightly west and you couldn't see down it anymore.

'I'll ride the train on to Yaqui and get some.'

Cole still held the Winchester exactly as he had held it when he was talking to the Sheltons. He was squinting into the sun as he looked southwest along the wash. His face, half shielded by his hat's brim, was without expression.

'I'll bring the horses back here,' I said, 'and if you ain't here, I'll follow you down the wash.'

Cole turned suddenly and walked off the bridge and began to edge down the side of the dry wash.

'You leave the wash,' I said. 'Leave me a sign.'

Cole didn't answer or look at me. He started walking southwest along the flat bottom of the wash, looking at the tracks in the dirt. I went back and got aboard the train.

We didn't get to Yaqui until after six that night. Stringer, being a deputy, could roust people around a little and, even though some of the stores were closed in Yaqui, I was on the way back to Chester by 8:15 with three horses and a pack mule carrying supplies. There was a good moon, and the stars were bright, and all I had to do was follow the tracks.

CHAPTER 32

When I got to the water tower, the moon was nearly down, but the sky to the east was still dark. I let the horses and the mule drink from a trough near the windmill. There was nothing moving in the wash. If I started down there now, in the dark, I couldn't read the tracks, and if Cole had left me a sign, I might not see it. This wasn't going to be a quarter-mile horse race. This would be a long ride. Long rides went better when you didn't hurry. I tethered the animals, gave them some feed, and ate a can of peaches. I sat down with my back against the railroad shed and slept for a while, facing east, so the sunrise would wake me up. Which it did.

It was slow going down the wash, trailing three animals. I thought about driving them ahead of me, but that would have wiped out any tracks that the Sheltons, and Cole, left. Next spring the wash would be roiling with water until summer. But right now it was dry as dust, with the little rivulet patterns of the spring torrent showing on the bottom. The hoofprints from the Sheltons' horses were clear enough, and among them I could see

Cole's boot prints. They had a twelve-hour start on me, but sooner or later I'd catch up with Cole, and then, sooner or later, we'd catch up with Allie.

I had matches wrapped up in oilcloth in my shirt pocket. I had a Winchester in a saddle scabbard under my left leg, and the eight-gauge under my right. I had two canteens slung over the saddle horn. I had a .45-caliber Colt on my belt and a Bowie knife. Wrapped in a slicker and tied behind my saddle was a change of clothes. Cole would have to make do with what he was wearing. I had ammunition and food and water and whiskey and a few sundries on the mule.

The tracks were clear enough. There was nothing out here and no reason for anybody to be here. Nobody else had ridden the wash for a long time. There were some coyote tracks mixed in, and some antelope spoor. As the wash turned west, I could feel the sun hard on my back. It was getting hot. The horses weren't tugging on the lead anymore. The mule had been on a lead all his life and the extra saddle mounts had fallen into his rhythm. I drank a little water. The sun was halfway up toward midday when the wash petered out onto a flat plain. The tracks stayed west and then got hard to follow in the scrub that covered the ground. I had to get off my horse to follow them, leading all four of the damned animals. Pretty soon they'd be riding me.

It was past midday when I came to a pile of stones about a foot high. I stopped and squatted and looked at it. Beside it, on the ground, was a smaller pattern of stones in the form of an arrow. It pointed south. I scattered the stones, remounted, and turned my animals south, and we moved on. I didn't need to track much anymore. I knew Cole would leave me directions. And he did. Some mesquite freshly cut. Some dry sticks pointing south, bigger growth with a prominent slash. In the late afternoon, I found him, near a shale outcropping, sitting on a rock, beside a marshy-looking water hole, with the Winchester in his lap, his boots off, and his feet in the water. He watched me ride up, trailing the animals.

'Everett,' he said.

'Virgil.'

'Might as well get down,' Cole said. 'We can camp here. Water's good, and' – he nodded at the outcropping – 'we can shelter a fire if we stay by the stone.'

I unloaded the mule and unsaddled the horses and put them on a loose tether so they could drink and forage for food among the scrub. Then I built a fire against the outcropping and put out food for supper, and squatted on my heels and started to cook. Cole never moved from where he sat with his feet in the water, until the thick slices of salt pork began to hiss in the frying pan. Then he put his boots on and came to the fire with a limp that barely showed. He poured himself some coffee.

'Whiskey in that saddlebag,' I said.

He got the bottle and poured some in his coffee.

'You?' he said.

I held out my coffee cup, and he poured some whiskey into it. Each of us took a sip, first blowing on the surface of the coffee so we wouldn't burn our lips.

'Stringer getting a posse up?' Cole said.

'Talking about it when I left Yaqui,' I said.

'You found my stones.'

'Yep.'

'Scatter the arrow?' Cole said.

'Yep.'

Cole sipped more of his coffee.

'Good,' he said after he swallowed. 'Don't want no god-damn herd of cowboys and hardware clerks stampedin' around out here. Getting in our way.'

When the salt pork had cooked nearly through, I dropped some biscuit dough into the grease and let it fry, and turned it once, and took the fried biscuits and the salt pork and put them into tin plates.

'They ahead of us?' I said.

'Yep. Probably widened the gap today. Me walking and all.'

'Twelve,' I said, 'fifteen hours.'

Cole nodded.

'They know we're behind them?' I said.

'Sheltons know me,' Cole said. 'They know I'll be coming.'

'We plannin' on stayin' the night here?' I said.

'Got to sleep,' Cole said. 'We ain't going to catch them today.'

I leaned back a little and stretched out my legs and drank some more coffee. Cole looked at the mule and the horses.

'Must have been tiresome,' Cole said, 'draggin' them three animals on a lead.'

'Some,' I said. 'Mule caught on pretty quick, and the horses got the idea in time.'

'Be easier now. I'll lead her horse, you lead the mule.'

I nodded. We ate our meal and drank coffee with whiskey and didn't say much. When it was dark, we let the fire die and settled to sleep between it and the rock, wrapped in strong-smelling saddle blankets.

'Got any thoughts where they might be headed?' I said to Cole.

'South,' Cole said.

CHAPTER 33

It was just after dawn on our third day, and the trail had turned straight west. Now and then, Cole would see a hoof print in among the ground cover. But mostly, we were able to follow them through horse droppings and the signs of campfires.

'I been thinking,' I said to Cole.

'Un-huh.'

He rode with his eyes on the ground, leading the saddle horse, with me trailing the mule.

'We're all the law there was in Appaloosa,' I said.

'Yep.'

'And now we ain't there.'

'Yep.'

'So,' I said. 'Now there ain't no law there.'

'Yep.'

'And that don' bother you?' I said.

Cole looked up from the tracking for a moment.

'No,' he said. 'It don't.'

We rode on: Cole, head down, looking at the ground; me riding beside him, looking at the landscape. The saddle horse trailing placidly behind him, the mule behind me. Neither of us said anything.

When we kicked up a jackrabbit, my hand went to my handgun, before I caught it. Cole never flinched. I'm not even sure he saw the rabbit. We kept on. We didn't hurry, but we didn't stop. Ahead, past the horizon above where our present direction would take us, there was a circular movement in the sky.

'Buzzards,' I said.

Cole looked up. His face showed nothing. We kept on. In maybe an hour, we came to where the buzzards were feeding. It was the carcass of a young buffalo, mostly bones now, and hooves. Most of what could be eaten had been. The buzzards flew up as we rode up, and landed again a few feet away. Cole ignored them. He got off his horse and went and squatted on his heels and looked at the remnants. The buzzards hopped restlessly just out of his reach. He paid no attention.

'Hide's gone,' he said.

I sat my horse and waited, looking at the landscape. Cole didn't need my help with the buffalo.

'Scapula's broke,' he said.

I looked down and could see that it was. Cole rummaged a little among the bones and the blood-soaked grass where the buffalo had fallen.

'Shot,' he said.

Cole opened his hand and showed me two big lead slugs, misshapen from shattering the scapula.

'Bigger'n a forty-five,' Cole said.

'Fifty, maybe.'

'Maybe one of them old Sharps buffalo guns,' Cole said.

The vultures edged closer. There were still a few scraps on the bones.

'I didn't see no sign of one,' I said, 'with the Sheltons.'

'Nope. Wouldn't take the hide, either.'

He was looking at the ground.

'See the horse tracks?' he said.

I rode nearer and wheeled around the dead animal, scattering the buzzards as I went.

'Not shod,' I said.

'And they bothered to skin it and take the hide,' Cole said.

'Indians.'

'Yep.'

I rode out a little way from the carcass, and in a slow wider circle, which infuriated the buzzards who had just lit there, after I'd scattered them in closer. On foot, Cole walked out toward where I was. I leaned forward in my saddle.

'Here's the shod hoofprints,' I said. 'And the unshod, mingled.'

Cole squatted, looking at the smudges in the dirt. Then he got down on his belly and put his face barely an inch away from the prints and looked, and slithered along like that, looking.

'Shod prints are older,' he said. 'Sides have begun to crumble a little. Unshod prints are over them. Fresher.'

I looked at the landscape again. Nothing moved but the unhappy buzzards.

'Kiowa?' I said.

'No way to say. There's some out here.'

'Could be hunters,' I said.

'Could be, but if they was just huntin' they'd take bones, ligaments, horns, teeth, everything. Here they just took the hide and meat.'

'No squaws,' I said.

Cole nodded.

'When you was with the Army,' he said, 'was the Kiowas hostile.'

'They were,' I said. 'But you know Indians. Yesterday they were, today maybe they ain't.'

'Can you tell how far behind the Sheltons they are?'

'Ain't that good,' Cole said.

'Can you tell how far ahead of us they are?'

'Carcass don't smell yet,' Cole said.

'Ain't much left that would smell,' I said.

'Blood would,' Cole said. 'Soaked in the ground.'

He stood and swung back up onto his horse.

'Best keep moving,' he said.

He kept looking at the ground as we rode on. I kept looking around us.

CHAPTER 34

We camped without a fire that night, in the bend of a small river, so that the water was on three sides. And we tethered the animals close.

'No coffee,' I said. 'But I still got whiskey.'

'It'll do,' Cole said.

We ate some beef jerky and cold fry biscuits and drank some whiskey.

'Indian sign turned off about five miles back,' Cole said. 'Sheltons are still going straight.'

'So they give up on the Sheltons.'

Or they had to stop and jerk that buffalo before it started to rot,' Cole said. 'Or they had something to do wherever they went and they'll come back. Them Kiowas know there's something ahead of 'em, and how many. It's just if they want to chase them down.'

'Sheltons got three good gun hands, plus Allie. You know how many Indians?'

'Can't say. They're riding too close, and we don't have time for me to get down and look close enough for long enough. There's more than two.'

Cole passed me the whiskey bottle and I drank some.

150

'You know if Allie can shoot?'

'Anybody can shoot,' Cole said. 'And hit something if it's close enough.'

'Think they'd give her a gun?'

'I don't think nothing,' Cole said. 'Can you stay awake until midnight?'

'Yes.'

'And I can stay awake from then to dawn,' Cole said. 'Wake me up.'

He rolled up in his saddle blanket and, as far as I could tell, went to sleep right away. I put the whiskey away and wrapped my saddle blanket around me, sat in the dark under the high stars with the shotgun across my lap, and listened to the sound of the river and the smell of the water and the grass mixed with the smell of horse blanket, and the night went its way. Halfway to dawn, I woke Cole. He came awake as instantly as he'd fallen asleep.

In the morning, the mule woke me up, nudging at me for its morning feed. We fed the stock and washed in the river and had a cold breakfast and moved on.

'Sheltons got to be heading someplace,' I said. 'They probably got some money before they started, but nobody's fool enough to pay them all. They got to deliver Bragg to collect the rest.'

'Be my suppose,' Cole said.

'So they're headin' someplace, and we're behind them,' I said. 'Good to know we ain't just wandering.'

Cole nodded, his eyes on the ground.

"Course it'd be even better to know where the someplace was.'

'Would,' Cole said.

It was late morning when Cole halted and bent out of his saddle, looking at the ground.

'Indians are back,' he said.

I moved up beside him and saw them, too. They had trailed in from the west and cut the Sheltons' tracks.

We moved on that way for a little, slowly, with Cole hanging out of the saddle, studying the tracks.

'They're following,' Cole said.

'Any better sense of how many?'

Cole studied the tracks as we rode.

After maybe a mile of silence, he said, 'Can't really tell much. Might be quite a few.'

By mid-afternoon the trail turned west, and by late afternoon we were climbing. We had to move the animals slower and rest them some. By dark, we were in the foothills of some mountains and the temperature was cooler. We camped under an overhang against the hillside, near a spring. There was grass. We let the animals graze on a long tether. We sat in the dark again that night and ate jerky and hardtack and drank some whiskey.

'We ain't going to be able to follow these tracks much more if they keep heading up,' I said.

'We can look for broken branches,' Cole said. 'Campfire ashes, the leavin's from a meal, horse droppings, maybe some human waste.'

'If they keep going straight,' I said. 'You got any idea where we are?'

'Two days southwest of Chester,' Cole said.

'You know what mountains these are?'

'Nope.'

'You think we're closing on them at all?' I said.

'Can't say, but I know Allie ain't much of a rider. She may slow them down.'

'What are we going to do about her?' I said.

'We'll figure that out when we get there,' Cole said.

'They'll use her as a shield, Virgil, why they brought her.'

''Course they will. Wouldn't you?'

There was no moon. The sky was clouded. With our blankets around us, we sat in near absolute darkness. We couldn't see each other. We didn't know where we were. There was only the sound of the animals eating grass, and trickling water, and our voices. It felt like being the only living human thing in the universe.

'Hard business,' I said. 'Hard business.'

'It's all hard business,' Cole said, 'what we do.'

'You all right?' I said.

Cole was silent for a time and then he said, 'All right?'

'How you feel,' I said. ''Bout Allie and all.'

Cole was silent again, and the silence seemed so long that I thought maybe he'd gone to sleep.

Then he said, 'Everett, we been together now awhile. Can't exactly say how long, but long. And

153

there ain't anyone I'd rather do this work with. You're as good as anybody I seen, 'cept maybe the Shelton boys . . . and me.'

'That's pretty good,' I said.

'And the reason you ain't as good as the Sheltons or me ain't got nothing to do with steady, or fast, or fortuitous.'

I knew he meant *fortitude*.

'The reason the above-named folks are better'n you,' Cole said, 'is 'cause you got feelin's.'

'Hell, Virgil, everybody got feelin's.'

'Feelin's get you killed,' Virgil said.

'You tellin' me you don't care about Allie right now?'

Again, there was silence. I could hear one of the horses snort, as if maybe he'd gotten an insect up his nose. It was a comforting sound in the vast, black silence. It sounded familiar and calm.

After a while Cole said, 'I cared about Allie in town. And I'll care about her when I get her back.'

'But right now?' I said.

I could feel Cole thinking it over.

'Gimme that bottle,' he said, and put his hand out and touched my leg so I knew where to hand him the bottle. I put the bottle in his hand and heard him drink. Then the bottle touched my leg again and I took it back and drank some.

'Right now,' Cole said, 'there's something runnin', and I'm trying to catch it.'

I heard him stir around as if to get more comfortable, and then he was silent. I had the first half of the night. I shifted my back a little against the boulder where we were, and sipped some whiskey and sat in the thick darkness and listened.

CHAPTER 35

The next morning, we went mostly on foot, leading the animals. We looked for any sign that would tell us they'd been there, and the sign was sparse. About mid-morning, we worked our way around a side of ledge to the top of a valley. In the bottom of the valley was a river that led out into the foothills and, beyond that, to the flatlands. In the flatland, on the south side of the river, was movement. We stopped at the top of the valley and looked at it.

I got a spyglass out of my saddlebag and handed it to Cole. He telescoped it open and looked down at the movement. His eyes weren't no better than mine. But it was his woman they took.

'Four riders,' Cole said after a while. 'And a pack animal. One of the riders is a woman.'

He handed me the glass and I looked. They were too far to make out that it was Allie, but who the hell else would it be.

'Picked up a third man,' I said. 'Musta been waiting someplace with the packhorse.'

Cole didn't answer. He sat motionless on his horse, staring down at the plain.

'We can work our way down to the river easy enough,' he said, 'without them seeing us.'

I lowered the glass.

'Then we can sit tight and rest the animals, and us, until the sun goes down and they make camp. Then we can ride out and get close.'

Below us, in the foothills to the north of the river, there was movement.

'That way, we can lay flat and get the lay of how things are,' Cole said. ''Fore we go in.'

I put the glass back up to my eye and looked at the movement in the foothills. It was Indians, riding close together among the pine trees, staying behind the hills. It was too hard to count through the glass with much accuracy. But I guessed twelve. I handed the glass to Cole and pointed. He studied the Indians without expression.

'Southern Cheyenne?' he said.

'Maybe,' I said. 'Maybe Kiowa. I think they're carrying them little medicine shields like Kiowas have.'

Cole looked some more.

'Might be,' he said. 'Make any difference?'

'Nope. Neither one of 'em likes us.'

'Got no reason to,' he said. 'How many you count?'

'Twelve.'

'About what I count,' Cole said. 'Maybe a few more.'

'They're doggin' those folks,' I said.

'Yep,' Cole said.

'They'll be a problem.'

'Speculate that they will,' Cole said. 'Nothin' we can do about it.'

'No,' I said.

'So we'll just keep doing what we're doing,' Cole said, and moved his horse forward and let it begin to pick its way down the side of the valley, with the extra saddle horse behind him.

I followed with the mule. As we got down into the valley, the Indians were out of sight behind the hills. We wouldn't see them again until we got out of the valley. Then we might see more of them than we wanted to. If the thought was bothering Cole, he didn't mention it. Nor did he show any sign of being in a hurry. He was going where he was going to go at the pace he needed to go at, and he was taking me with him.

CHAPTER 36

We camped at the bottom of the foothills, just before we reached the plain, next to the river, in a grove of trees. It was still daylight, and we had an early, cold supper. No whiskey this day.

'I need some coffee,' I said.

'Yes,' Cole said.

'We get through with this and I'm going to drink ten cups,' I said. 'For breakfast.'

'Won't be dozin' much that day,' Cole said.

The animals grazed in the shade. We took turns washing ourselves and our clothes in the river, and spread the wet clothes on the grass at the edge of the trees, away from the river, to dry in the sun. I had a change of clothes. But Cole didn't. While his clothes dried, Cole walked around in a pair of clean drawers I gave him, with his gun belt on.

'Them Indians show up now, Virgil, you ain't gonna have to shoot 'em,' I said. 'They gonna die from laughin'.'

At sundown, with clean clothes, Cole's nearly dry, we set out along the river as quiet as we could. The sun was down, but the moon wasn't up yet, and all the light there was lingered from the set sun. Cole went first. He had the lead from the riderless horse tied to his saddle, and his Winchester out of the sheath and cocked. I rode the same way, with the mule. I was listening so hard that I was getting tired, like it was a muscular effort. To our right, the river was still running turbulent out of the mountains. Ahead of us, I knew, it would broaden and meander on the flat plain. Aside from the river, the only sounds we heard were our own as we moved west on the south side of the river. The land flattened, and the pines gave way to cottonwoods along the river. After another hour or so of soft riding, Cole stopped and sat still. I sat beside him.

'Smell it,' he said quietly.

'Camp fire,' I said.

We moved on, slower, staying close to the edge of the river, among the cottonwoods. In the moonlight, we could see up ahead where the river bent in an almost U-shaped meander, and on the tip of the point of land it created, we could see the fire. We stood still. Occasionally, we could see movement as someone passed between us and the fire. We tied the animals and went forward as quiet as we could move. The tree cover gave out maybe fifty yards from the camp. But it was close enough. We could both see that it was the Sheltons. I took the glass out and handed it to Cole. He lengthened it and put it to his eye. He slowly swept the glass over the campsite. Without the glass, I could see that there were three people sitting by the fire with a bottle. None was Allie. I looked around. Near the river, there was a cluster of brush, and behind it, in the river, near the bank, there was movement. Cole settled the glass on it. I waited. As Cole watched, I heard the sound of a woman laughing. It was so unexpected that I almost didn't know what the sound was. Cole watched for a time. Then, without a sound, he handed me the glass. I adjusted it a little and brought Allie and Ring Shelton into focus. They were standing thigh-deep in the river. They were naked. I put the glass down and collapsed it. I didn't look at Cole. We heard Allie laugh again, and we saw their indistinct shapes come out of the river and sink to the ground behind the brush cluster, and we couldn't see them. But in the still, night air, we could hear them. I turned and walked several feet back toward the horses and stopped, and walked back, and stood next to Cole.

'Along the river,' Cole said. 'Beyond the camp.'
The Indians had found the Sheltons.
'Must have been a ford downstream,' I said. 'They went on down the north side of the river, and forded and came back.'
'Bring the animals up,' Cole said.
'Mule, too?'
'Yep.'
I turned and went. It took a little to maneuver three horses and a mule through the trees quietly, but the sound of the river helped cover our sounds.

When I got back, the Indians were in the camp, all of them armed. Most of them with Winchesters. All of them sitting their horses, looking silently down at the three men around the campfire. Cole had retreated a few yards back, in among the trees. Three of them detached from the main body and walked their horses over to the brush where Ring and Allie were. They looked down solemnly for a while and then one of them said something to the other two and all three laughed. The first rider was carrying an old Sharps rifle, that must have killed the buffalo we found. He gestured Ring and Allie should join the others. Ring bent over and picked up his pants. He looked silently back at the Indian with the Sharps rifle as he slowly slid one leg on, then the other, and buttoned them up. Allie bent down to pick up her dress, and the Indian leaned from his saddle, with the rifle in one hand, steady on Ring, and took the dress away and flung it into the river. When Ring had finished buttoning, he gestured again with the rifle, toward the campfire. One of the other Indians jumped down from his horse and picked up one of Allie's undergarments. He tied it carefully onto his lance and jumped back up astride the horse and waved the lance triumphantly over his head. All of the Indians laughed. I was pretty sure they were Kiowas. Ring and Allie walked to the fire. Allie stood naked in the middle of four white men and maybe a dozen bucks.

'We'll watch a bit, see if they got bad intentions.'

'And if they do?'

'We'll shoot a couple,' Cole said, 'many as we can 'fore they scatter.'

'What about the whites?' I said.

'They'll run for the tree cover,' Cole said. 'Ring and Mackie will both know.'

'And then what?'

'And then we'll see,' Cole said. 'Make sure them horses is tied secure 'fore we shoot.'

I did, and then went back to him. Bragg was holding the whiskey. One of the Indians leaned out of his saddle and took the bottle from Bragg's hands and raised it to his mouth and drank some and passed the bottle to the buck next to him.

'Any of you bucks speak English,' Bragg said.

The Indian with the Sharps rifle turned his horse toward where Bragg was standing and put the muzzle of the rifle against Bragg's forehead, then put his hand to his own mouth and made a silencing gesture. Bragg stood frozen. Four of the Indians dismounted and began going through the Shelton party's belongings.

I whispered to Cole, 'We start shooting, they'll scatter.'

'They won't charge us.'

'Indians ain't stupid. They can't see us. They don't know how many we are. They'll scatter and regroup on the other side of that rise.'

'And they won't just run off,' Cole said.

'No,' I said. 'There's a lot of stuff here they want.

Probably includin' Allie. They'll settle in behind the rise, see what's what.'

Cole and I looked for a moment at the low hill half a mile from the river.

'Don't think they ain't good fighters,' I said. 'They can ride like hell, and they can shoot, and they ain't afraid to die. Buck with the Sharps Rifle probably runs things.'

'We let 'em take what they want,' Cole said. ''Cept Allie.'

I nodded, which was a waste of time. Cole wasn't looking at me. He was studying the Indians, who were collecting the weapons and the whiskey. They loaded these and some foodstuffs into two big bags on a pack animal, then they gathered the horses. Sharps Rifle said something to one of the horse gatherers, and he nodded and saddled one of the horses. The rest were herded to the back of the group, ready to be driven ahead of them when they left. The saddle horse was handed to Sharps Rifle. He took the lead in one hand and, holding the rifle in the other, moved his horse with the pressure of his knees away from Bragg and stopped him in front of Allie. He jerked his head at the horse.

'No,' she said.

Standing naked among all the men, her body looked small and white. The Indian gestured with his rifle. Allie seemed to get smaller; she stepped back as if to shield herself behind Ring Shelton. He didn't move. He simply watched the Indian.

Sharps Rifle said something again, and two Indians jumped down. One of them tossed a blanket around Allie's shoulders. She clutched it around her as if it were armor. Then the two Indians picked her up and put her on the horse.

'Shoot the packhorse,' Cole said. 'We'll need the weapons.'

Then he raised the Winchester and shot Allie's horse out from under her. Before the animal had floundered down, he had shot the Indian with the Sharps rifle in the middle of the chest. I killed the pack animal and put a bullet into the Indian who'd been holding it. The rest flattened themselves over their horses' necks, and hanging down on the side away from the gunfire drove them in a flat-out run toward the low hill. Cole and I each managed to knock down another horse, but in both cases the rider was up and behind another Indian before the horse had died.

The Shelton horses, waiting to be driven, had spooked and were strung out at a gallop along the river, straight west. The Shelton brothers dove flat behind the dead packhorse. Mackie pulled a knife from his boot and cut the pack bags loose, Bragg and the other man came at a dead run toward us in the woods. Allie struggled away from her dead horse and followed them, hanging on to her blanket. Mackie took one pack bag and Ring took the other, and they sprinted for the woods as well. The Indians didn't shoot; they were heading for the hill. There'd be plenty of time to kill us, if the Indians decided they could.

The Indians went behind the rise, out of sight. Mackie cut open the pack bags, and he and Ring got their guns out, rifles and sidearms. Bragg and the fourth man got theirs out as well. When this was done, Ring straightened and looked at us.

'Knew you'd be after us,' Ring said.

Cole nodded.

'Kiowa?' Cole said to Ring.

'Think so. They got them funny little shields,' Ring said. 'How many horses you got?'

'Three and a pack mule,' Cole said.

Ring looked at me.

'Everett,' he said.

Mackie nodded at me.

Allie was crouched near us with her blanket around her. Bragg had flattened out on the ground with a Winchester, facing toward the hill where the Indians had gone.

'This here's my cousin Russell,' Ring said. 'Russell can shoot a little.'

Russell nodded, looking off toward where the Indians had vanished behind the rise. He was a small, wiry man with a big Adam's apple and not much hair.

'First thing,' Cole said. 'While we got them hostiles to deal with, it ain't a good idea for us to be shootin' each other.'

'There's a town we was heading for, 'bout two days ride,' Ring said. 'Without pushing the horses,

I say we put our troubles aside until the day after we get there.'

'Your word?' Cole said.

'My word.'

Cole nodded.

'Everett?' he said.

'Twenty-four hours?'

Ring nodded.

'Fine,' I said.

'Okay,' Cole said. 'Mackie, you got any clothes in there to cover Allie up?'

'None a hers,' Mackie said. 'You remember she come along sort of sudden.'

'Got some spare pants in there,' Russell said. 'I seen them Indians pack 'em.'

He felt around in the bag and came out with the pants and gave them to Allie. I gave Allie my clean shirt. Clutching the blanket around her she stood and looked for a place to change.

Cole said, 'We seen pretty much everything you got, Allie. No reason to go hiding it now.'

Without looking at him, she went behind some bushes and came out a minute later, looking silly but dressed. The pants were too big. She rolled the bottoms and I cut her some rope to make a belt. I was at least twice her size. My shirt billowed around her. The sleeves were too long to roll. I cut them off for her at about the elbows.

'Fire's dying down,' Russell said. 'Ain't much moon. I can snake out there and get them moccasins off one of them bucks you shot.'

'I can't wear those.'

I said, 'You don't want to be walking around barefoot, Allie.'

'We can't spare no shooters,' Ring said.

'I can get 'em,' Russell said. 'I don't make much of a target.'

He eased out from the trees on his stomach and scooted on his belly toward the nearest corpse. He could go like hell on his stomach. He came back with the moccasins.

'Fit anybody,' Russell said. 'Just wrap the laces around your legs.'

The moccasins had been greased to keep them flexible and to repel water. Allie looked like she wouldn't take them, then she did and put them on and wrapped the lacings. She looked preposterous. But she was dressed. Being dressed seemed to pick her up a little.

'What are we going to do?' she said.

Her voice wasn't very big, and it had no reason to be. I noticed she put the question to a spot about halfway between Ring and Virgil.

'We're workin' on that,' Ring said. 'Sit over there.'

Allie looked at Cole. He was looking elsewhere. Allie went and sat against the foot of a tree near the horses and the mule. Mackie picked up his Winchester and moved to the edge of the woods away from Bragg. Russell settled in near the middle of our little perimeter. Cole and Ring and I sat on our heels between Russell and Mackie, and looked out of the shelter of the trees at the low rise across from us, and not very far.

'Think they'll come at us?' Ring said.

'Nope,' Cole said. 'Everett?'

'No,' I said. 'They won't. Not until they know what we are and how many. They'll put someone upriver and downriver within shouting distance, and they'll watch us from behind the hill.'

'They know we ain't got enough horses,' Ring said.

'They don't know that; we could have brought extra. In the morning, they'll send someone upriver a ways to track us, see how many we are, then they'll know we're short some horses.'

'Yours'll probably come drifting back,' Cole said.

'Indians will kill them if they do,' I said.

''Less they don't see 'em,' Ring said.

'They'll see 'em,' Cole said.

Ring nodded.

'They will,' he said. 'Won't they.'

'And noon tomorrow, when the trackers come back, they'll know how many we are and how many horses we got.'

'Nobody can read sign like an Indian,' Cole said.

''Less they drink up all the whiskey tonight,' Ring said.

I shook my head.

'Everett's right,' Cole said. 'These are fighters. They ain't going to get drunk in the middle of a fight.'

'So I guess we got to dig in here and await developments,' Ring said.

169

'Anybody see if they got food?' I said.

'Didn't see none,' Ring said.

Cole shook his head no.

'Butchered that buffalo a ways back,' he said. 'Musta cooked it, probably still got some left.'

'There's about ten of 'em got to eat,' I said.

'Thirteen.' Ring said. 'There was fifteen when they arrived. You killed two.'

'Food might work for us or against us,' Cole said. 'They get hungry and they got someplace else to get it, they might go there. They ain't, it'll make 'em more vigilant, trying to get ours.'

I think he meant vigorous. But Ring and I both knew what he meant.

'We got the river behind us,' Ring said. 'And we back up a little to the end of this point, we'll have it on three sides.'

'Can't watch 'em too good from there,' I said.

'Got a shovel on the mule,' Cole said. 'We can dig us in a little back there, and pull down some trees and branches around, shield the horses. Couple of us stay up here, if they come at us and we need to, we can pull everybody back into the redoubt.'

'Now?' I said.

'I'd say so,' Cole said.

CHAPTER 37

'We can build a fire,' Bragg said. 'Ain't like they don't know we're here.'

We had dug us a small hollow by the river, and dragged some brush and tree limbs around.

'Sure can,' Ring said. 'And then maybe cook a little something over it.'

'I could use some coffee,' Bragg said.

'So build the fire and make some coffee,' Ring said. 'And if they decide to sneak in closer, maybe swim the river and shoot at the fire from behind us, they might miss you.'

'You think they'd do that?' Bragg said.

Ring glanced at Cole.

'What's that thing you always used to say, Virgil? Read it in some book?'

'Clausewitz,' Cole said. 'Clausewitz says you gotta plan for what your enemy can do, not what you think he'll do.'

'Fuck Clausewitz,' Bragg said.

But he didn't start a fire.

'Everett and I will go up front now.'

'Be sure and let Mackie know it's you,' Ring said. 'You know how quick he is.'

Bent nearly double, Cole and I went through the cottonwoods toward the fallen tree behind which Mackie and Russell were watching.

When we were maybe a hundred feet away, Cole said, 'Virgil Cole, Mackie.'

'Come on,' Mackie said.

We dropped to our knees and crept to the watch spot.

'You boys can head back now, get some sleep,' Cole said.

They left us without a word. Both of them moved very quietly in the woods. Ahead of us, the land was treeless. The Sheltons' fire had died away entirely. The moon was already declining but still bright enough to fill the land between the woods and the low hill with pallid emptiness. Nothing moved. There was no sound except the water behind us. The sky was vast and dark. There were stars, but they seemed pitiless.

'They'll come in the morning,' Cole said.

'Not right at us,' I said.

'No. I figure they'll send some riders around out of rifle range and cross the river and come back up behind us. They'll wait for the trackers to go upstream and find our trail. See who we are, how many we are.'

'Woods aren't that thick,' I said. 'In the day, they'll get a fair idea even 'fore the trackers come back.'

'We can try to keep down,' Cole said. 'Not move around.'

'When the trackers come back, they'll know anyway,' I said.

'Still ain't good battlefield for 'em,' Cole said. 'They got to cross that open land between us and the hill.'

'Or swim the river.'

'Either way, they got to come at us with no cover and six of us shooting.'

'They know that,' I said.

'Expect they do.'

'If they do, then we're back to seeing how long they'll sit there,' I said. 'We got all the water we need, and we got some food.'

'Might be smart to parcel it out small,' Cole said.

'Might be.'

'We don't know what they got,' Cole said.

'Or how far they'd have to go to get it.'

'Water's not a problem for them, either.'

'Nope,' I said. 'They just go down the river out of range and get it.'

Behind us, a small voice said, 'Virgil.'

'Yes, Allie,' Virgil said.

'Can I come up and sit with you and Everett?'

'Yep.'

She came up crouching, in her ridiculous clothes, looking very small, and sat cross-legged on the ground between us.

'You ever fire a pistol,' Cole said.

'No.'

'Best you learned. Everett, you got that little hideout dingus you usually carry?'

'I do,' I said, and took an over under derringer out of the side pocket of my pants.

I broke it open, took out the two .45 cartridges, and closed the weapon.

'It's unloaded now,' I said. 'But pretend it isn't.'

I handed it to her. She handled it as if it were some vile reptile.

'Just a piece of equipment, Allie,' I said. 'Like a cherry pitter. Won't do anything 'less you operate it.'

'It's not very heavy,' she said.

'It'll be a little heavier with the bullets in it.'

I had her dry fire it a few times, then I took it and reloaded it and gave it back to her.

'I . . . what am I supposed to do with it?'

'Keep it with you,' I said.

'Indians win this,' Cole said, 'cock that thing, put it in your mouth, pull the trigger.'

'Kill myself?'

''Less you want to be the bottom squaw in some buck's string,' Cole said.

'Oh, God,' she said.

Neither Cole or I said anything. I don't imagine Cole could think of anything to say, either. Awkwardly, Allie put the derringer in the pocket of her too-big pants. The three of us sat, looking out over the short stretch of empty prairie.

Finally Allie said, 'I'm sorry, Virgil.'

Cole didn't speak.

'I don't know what to say, Virgil. I . . . how are we going to make this right?'

Cole stayed silent, looking toward where the Kiowas were.

'I was so alone,' Allie said, 'and Bragg was . . . Ring protected me, and he told his brother to protect me. And they both did.'

Cole didn't turn his head.

'So you fuck Mackie, too?' he said.

'I . . . no . . . It was Ring. Ring was in charge. What was I supposed to do?' Allie said.

Cole didn't say anything else. I didn't want any part of this and had nothing to say.

'I was alone . . . I want to fix this between us, between you and Ring.'

Cole turned his head slowly and looked at her in the faint light.

'I'll think about that another time,' Cole said. 'Right now, I'm thinking about Indians.'

CHAPTER 38

At first light, we spotted the tracker. He swung out in a big arc from behind the hill, staying out of rifle range, and headed upstream. Another rider came out on the other side, described the same wide arc out of range, and headed downstream.

'He ain't a tracker,' Cole said. 'They come from down there they know we didn't.'

'He'll cross downstream, come up for a look on the other side of the river,' I said.

'And we just sit here?' Bragg said.

'Not if you got a better plan,' Cole said.

'Maybe we send somebody out after them two bucks,' Bragg said. 'Got 'em isolated from the rest, kill 'em off, improve our odds.'

'Ain't a bad idea,' Ring said. ''Course them other Kiowas up there will see us send somebody, so they'll send somebody, too. So our man is outnumbered two to one.'

'Maybe our man can kill them both. We got some gun hands here.'

'Maybe,' Ring said. 'Which one you want to follow? Upstream or down?'

176

Bragg was silent. Then he shook his head.

'Might make a fire this morning,' I said. 'It won't stand out so much in the day.'

'Indians can't get close enough to shoot,' Cole said, 'in the daylight.'

We made our fire, and we all had coffee and fried salt pork. Coffee made me feel better. In about an hour, we saw one of the Indians on the other side of the river, squatting beside a big rock, looking at our campsite. About mid-morning we saw the upstream Indian come back, swinging wide away from our guns and disappearing behind the hill. When we looked again, the one across the river was gone. After that, nothing. We sat with our weapons, watching the hill. Nobody appeared. No sound drifted down across the grassland. Nothing happened. We drank some more coffee and ate some jerky and hardtack. We dipped the hardtack in the coffee to soften it. We took turns sleeping. For supper, Allie made fry biscuits. We ate them with salt pork and coffee and hardtack. We dipped our hardtack. We took turns sleeping.

On the second day of this, Bragg said to us, 'How do we know they're still there?'

'We don't,' Cole said.

'How we going to find out?' Bragg said.

No one said anything for a time, then I said, 'I'm going to ride up and see.'

All of them looked at me. I thought Cole was going to say something. But he didn't. Instead, he nodded. I got up and went to the brush-and-branches pen we'd made and saddled my horse. I put the Winchester in its saddle sleeve, checked my Colt and holstered it, picked up the shotgun and got on my horse.

'Don't go no further than you have to,' Cole said. 'I can cover you about halfway there. All we need to know is that they didn't keep the hill between us and skedaddle.'

I nodded. Cole picked up his rifle and settled in on his stomach with his Winchester. Ring did the same thing.

'We'll do what we can,' Ring said.

'Minute you see an Indian,' Cole said, 'you turn and run for the woods.'

I nodded again. Then I turned my horse's head and clucked and nudged him with my knee and we rode out of the woods and onto the short-grass open land. The sun was high and steady. I could smell the river and the grass. The horse was frisky from standing around in the woods. He capered a couple of times as we moved into the sun. I held him to a walk. There was no reason to hurry. Nothing was moving but me. The only sound was the horse walking. I had the shotgun resting across my saddle in front of me. It was cocked. As we walked toward the hill, the horse kicked up some grasshoppers and they jumped frantically in front of us. The horse tossed his head and blew a couple of times. I knew he wanted to run. I smiled a little to myself. Hell, so did I. We were almost out of range of the woods. At this distance, even for Cole, hitting what you were aiming at would be mostly luck. I kept riding slowly toward the hill. Nothing moved. Some more grasshoppers jumped around in front of us as we walked. The grass smell was strong. I didn't smell the river anymore. I could feel the hard sun on my back. We were almost to the foot of the hill. Out of rifle range. I was on my own. I stopped the horse for a moment and looked up the easy slope. Nothing moved. Then it did.

A young Indian was sitting his horse on the top of the hill. He was bare-chested, wearing leggings and moccasins. There were eagle feathers in his long hair. Not much of a war bonnet. He was not yet a significant chief, but he'd earned some feathers. His horse was a big buckskin with a light mane. It wasn't an Indian pony. He'd probably stolen it from the Army. There were white and colored beads in a tight collar around his neck, and in several looped necklaces on his chest. In the center, there was a kidney-shaped silver medallion. The lower half of his face was painted vermillion, with black paint on his cheeks and around his eyes. His eyelids were vermillion. He looked straight down at me. I looked up at him. There was contact, like looking at a wolf or a cougar and seeing not just the animal but its actual living self looking out at you. I should have turned the horse and headed back. But I didn't. I couldn't turn on him and run. I sat my horse with the shotgun across my saddle and waited.

In a moment, the other Indians came up behind him on the top of the hill and stopped and sat silently in a row maybe a horse's length behind him. My horse swished his tail at a fly. I waited. The young Indian began to ride slowly down the hill toward me. He sat his horse bareback. There was no bridle, merely a length of rope tied to the buckskin's jaw. I sat. The Indian came slowly. He was looking at me, and I at him. In his right hand he carried a Winchester. There were bullets in a looped belt around his waist. He carried a knife on the same belt. His eyes were dark brown and full of energy. I could see that the Winchester was cocked. He could see that the shotgun was cocked. My shotgun, resting on my saddle horn, was pointing to my left. He moved his horse to my right. I turned the shotgun. He seemed almost to smile. He shifted the Winchester to his left hand, holding it with the butt on his thigh and the barrel pointing up. I nodded and did the same with the shotgun. Again, he might have smiled. We were almost side by side now, headed in opposite directions. Then we were side by side, our horses standing head to tail. The Indian reached out carefully and put his right hand on my right shoulder. We sat for a fraction, as if all of time had come to a point on that contact.

Then he took his hand away and whirled his horse and whooped something in Kiowa and set the horse at a hard gallop up the hill. As he came toward them, the other Indians yelled and whooped and waved their weapons. When the young Indian reached the top of the hill, he spun his horse, making him rear and paw the air with his front feet as he did so. Then he set the horse back down on solid ground and looked down at me once more. A second Indian rode out beside him and planted a lance in the ground. It was the one with Allie's undergarment tied to it. Several of the Indians shouted in Kiowa, and then there was laughter. The young Indian with the vermillion jaw turned his horse and disappeared over the crest of the hill, and the other Indians followed him. I could hear their hooves going down the other side.

I nudged my horse forward and we went up the hill, my shotgun still pointing up, the butt still resting on my thigh. At the top of the hill, I looked down at a flat prairie that stretched to the horizon. Below me, the Kiowas were riding away at a comfortable pace.

CHAPTER 39

Beauville wasn't much. It wasn't even Appaloosa. But it was a railhead, where cattle driven up from Texas could load onto trains that would bring them to Omaha or Chicago. And being a railhead, it was livelier than it had any right to be otherwise.

We dragged into Beauville two days after my coup had been counted by the buck with the vermillion chin; we were tired, out of coffee, and short of most everything else. The horses were tired. The mule was tired. And we were tired. Allie, straggle-haired and badly dressed, dusty and sweat-streaked like the rest of us, looked especially tired. There was a hotel on the one street, and a bank, and a restaurant in a tent, and six saloons. At the far end of the street, there were a few small, unpainted houses. The train station, surrounded by cattle pens, was the grandest building in town. There was even a little steeple on it, with a big clock. According to the clock, it was 2:41. Behind the station was the city marshal's office and jail. 'This time tomorrow,' Ring said.

'This time,' Cole said.

'We'll ride on down to the station,' Ring said. 'You, too, Bragg. If the money's there, our deal is up. If the money's not there, we gonna be asking you where it is.'

'It'll be there,' Bragg said. He nodded at us. 'What about them?'

'Our deal covers them,' Ring said. He looked at Cole.

'That gonna be a problem?' Ring said.

'Might be,' Cole said.

Ring nodded.

'How about the woman?' he said. 'She a problem?'

'Might be,' Cole said.

'Well,' Ring said. 'Won't be a problem till tomorrow afternoon.'

He nudged his horse forward. His brother followed. Bragg trailed along, and Russell behind him. Allie sat uncertainly on her horse, near me.

'Lets head down to the hotel, Allie,' I said. 'Get you a room.'

'How about you two?' she said.

'I'll bunk in with Everett,' Cole said.

It was between cattle drives, and the hotel was nearly empty. We washed and slept and sent our clothes to the Chinaman. It was after dark when Cole and I went down to the saloon and Allie joined us. The hotelkeeper's wife had found her some clothes, probably from one of the whores who worked in the hotel, and Allie looked pretty good again.

It wasn't much of a saloon, two long planks set

183

on whiskey barrels. The whiskey sat in bottles on a table behind. We had a drink, including Allie, who drank hers in very small sips.

'Will the Sheltons stick to the truce?' I said.

'Ring's word is good,' Cole said.

'And so is ours,' I said.

'Yes.'

We were quiet. The hotelkeeper's wife came to the table.

'You folks hungry, we got some stew and some fresh bread,' she said. 'I baked it today.'

'How 'bout the stew?' Cole said.

'Been simmerin' 'bout six years,' the woman said. 'Just keep dishing it out and addin' in stuff.'

We ordered some.

'What are we going to do?' Allie said.

'We'll wait until tomorrow afternoon,' Cole said. 'Then we'll take Bragg back.'

'I meant us, Virgil,' she said.

I started to get up.

'I'll have a drink at the bar,' I said.

Cole put his hand on my arm.

'Sit,' he said.

'Does Everett have to be here, Virgil?' Allie said.

'Yep.'

I wasn't comfortable with it. But staying might not be a bad idea. If Allie started talking about us at her half-constructed house that rainy day, I would want to be around to see that the story got told adequately.

'Ring forced me to do that with him,' Allie said.

'Nope,' Cole said.

'He did, Virgil, I swear he did.'

Cole shook his head.

'I seen what I seen,' he said.

'I was afraid,' Allie said. 'I was doing what I had to do to stay alive.'

'He wouldn'ta killed you,' Cole said. 'He'd just trail you along with him till he didn't need you no more.'

'Maybe you know that,' Allie said. 'But I didn't know it, Virgil. And the other men. I was a woman alone with four terrible men.'

Cole drank some whiskey and stared into the glass and didn't say anything for a while.

Then he said to me, 'Tomorrow this time we'll have settled things with the Sheltons. If Ring kills me, you think she'll go off with him, Everett?'

'I think Allie needs to be with a man,' I said.

'You bastard,' Allie said. 'Don't listen to him, Virgil. The sonova bitch tried to put his hands on me one day when I was showing him our house.'

Cole looked at me.

'No, Virgil,' I said. 'I didn't.'

Cole looked at me for a moment longer. I looked back. Then he looked back into his whiskey glass.

'No, Allie,' he said. 'Everett didn't do that.'

'He's lying, Virgil. You believe him and not me?'

Cole studied the surface of his drink. He nodded his head slowly.

'That is correct,' he said.

'You men. You always stick together, don't you. What chance has a woman got, alone?'

Cole finished his drink and poured himself another. The hotelkeeper's wife brought us food. We all ate some and were quiet while we did. It was better than fried salt pork and hardtack.

'Well, if it'll help you feel easy,' Cole said after a time, 'nobody's killed me yet, and I don't think Ring can do it, either.'

'Why do you have to face him?'

'He's got my prisoner.'

'Can't you get the local marshal or whoever to help you?'

'Maybe,' Cole said. 'Either way, he's got my lawful prisoner.'

'And you just have to get him back,' Allie said.

'He's my lawful prisoner,' Cole said.

'And that's all there is to it?'

'I'm a lawman,' Cole said.

'And that's all you are?' Allie said.

'Mostly,' Cole said.

CHAPTER 40

After we ate, Cole and I went out and sat in a couple of chairs in front of the hotel. It was dark now, and the street traffic was mostly rail hands and cowboys heading for the saloons, and now and then a whore hurrying to work. Allie had gone back up to her room without speaking to us again. The night insects were making noise. I could hear the sound of a bad piano somewhere up the street.

'What happened at the house?' Cole said to me.

'I didn't make no advance at Allie,' I said.

'I believe it. I tole you that already. But I'd like to know what transacted.'

I told him. He nodded slowly as he listened. If he felt anything, he didn't show it. He sat with his chair tilted back, looking up through the clear night at the stars. After a while, he shook his head as if answering a question no one had asked.

'I never met no woman like her,' he said.

I was quiet.

'Mostly, I been with whores, and some squaws.'

Cole took out a cigar and lit it, turning it in the match flame, and got it going good and even.

187

'She talks good and dresses nice, and she's good-looking,' Cole said.

He took in some cigar smoke and blew it out and watched it thin out and disappear in the night air.

'She can play the piano, and she cooks nice, and she's very clean.'

Cole's voice was quiet in the near darkness. He was listing assets, I thought, deciding whether to buy.

'But,' Cole said, 'it appears she'll fuck anything ain't gelded.'

I shook my head.

'I ain't sure that's quite right,' I said.

'What do you think's right?'

'I think she wants to be with the boss stallion,' I said.

'Ain't but one stallion in a herd,' Cole said.

'At a time,' I said.

Cole smoked his cigar quietly for a time.

'So when I'm around she loves me,' Cole said.

'I think so,' I said.

'But I ain't around and you are, she loves you.'

'Probably ain't love,' I said.

'And when neither one of us is around, she loves Ring.'

'Again, I ain't sure I'd say love.'

'She love me?' Cole said.

'I can't say that she don't,' I said. 'You?'

Cole's voice sounded a little hoarse to me. Maybe he was embarrassed. I wasn't sure. I'd never seen him embarrassed.

'I think she does,' he said.

'You're the one should know,' I said.

He smoked some more of his cigar, holding the tip up and exhaling past it so he could see the smoke.

'That thing with Ring,' Cole said. 'It sticks in my throat, Everett. I can't seem to swallow it.'

'Sticks in mine, too,' I said.

He puffed his cigar.

'You know she takes a bath every evenin'?' he said. ''Fore she goes to bed.'

It was very dark, and I could only see Cole's face a little in the coal-oil light that came out of the hotel.

'I like bein' with her,' he said.

'Nothin' against it,' I said.

'No. I just got to get past the Ring business.'

'Might not be the last time,' I said.

'Be the last time with Ring,' Cole said.

A single horse and rider walked down the street in front of us, the horse's hooves making a kind of slurred sound in the dirt, the saddle creaking gently, a quiet sound of harness metal.

'Gonna talk with the town marshal tomorrow?' I said.

'Yep. Got no objection to help.'

'And if he's no help?'

'We done it by ourselves before,' Cole said.

'We're going up against Ring because of Bragg,' I said.

'Can't be a lawman and let somebody come take your prisoner,' Cole said.

'Nothin' personal.'

'Nope. Business.'

'We done pretty good over time, Virgil, 'cause it's never been personal. Always just a job.'

'It's always been the law, Everett. It's got to be the law. People like us got to have the law and got to do it by the law. You understand that, Everett. Otherwise you're just a damn shooter. Nothin' to prevent you from killin' anybody.'

'And that's how it is this time, too,' I said.

'That's how it is every time,' Cole said.

CHAPTER 41

In the morning, Cole and I walked down to the marshal's office and found Russell Shelton sitting at a desk in front of the single jail cell, wearing a marshal's badge.

'Russ,' Cole said.

'Virgil,' Russell said, 'Everett.'

'Didn't known you worked here,' I said.

'It's family,' Russell said. 'Ring 'n me 'n Mackie sorta take turns at it.'

'We're here looking for our prisoner,' Cole said.

'Got no prisoners here, Virgil.'

Cole nodded.

'I'm guessing you ain't gonna aid us in apprehending him,' he said, 'neither.'

'You really ain't a marshal here,' Russell said. 'You're only a marshal in Appaloosa.'

'You know where I can find Bragg?'

'He's with Ring,' Russell said, 'and Mackie.'

'And where would they be?' Cole said.

'I got to tell you boys,' Russell said. 'I got nothin' against either one of you. And I got a good feelin' about how you helped us out with them Kiowas.'

'Where's Bragg?' Cole said.

191

'I'm gonna be with Ring and Mackie,' Russell said. 'We're family. We grew up like brothers.'

'Yep. Where are they?'

'Ring says he don't want this thing to drag on. Him and Mackie and Bragg'll be at the stockyards at two forty-one today by the depot clock. I'll be there, too.'

'See you there,' Cole said, and turned and walked out of the office.

I stayed a minute.

'You got them boots for Allie,' I said.

Russell nodded. I reached over the desk and we shook hands.

'Be better you boys went on back to Appaloosa,' Russell said.

'I know,' I said, and followed Cole out of the office.

He was leaning his backside against a hitching rail, looking at the street. The sky was dark with clouds.

'Might as well walk down there, get the lay of the land,' he said.

'Might as well.'

We walked the dirt street toward the stockyards. It was a shabby town, shacks mostly, some tents. Only real buildings were the hotel and the railroad station. Even the bank looked kind of flimsy.

'They could put some people behind some of these shacks,' I said. 'Try to pick us off while we're walking to the yards.'

Cole shook his head.

'Sheltons'll come straight at us,' he said.

'Bragg?' I said.

'We'll need to keep an eye out for Bragg,' Cole said.

The stock pens were mostly empty. A couple dozen white-faced steers jostled each other in the pen nearest the station. There were two stockmen leaning on a rail, chewing tobacco and watching them. A windmill turned at the far end of the yards, pumping water into the drinking troughs. Beside it was a weathered, gap-sided feed shed, raw boards nailed up and bleached by sun.

'We'll be coming from here,' Cole said. 'Shelton's'll be there, by the shed.'

'How do you know,' I said.

'Where I'd be. If they don't knock us down with the first volley, they can get behind it,' Cole said.

He looked at the sky.

'Sun ain't gonna be an issue,' he said.

'Probably gonna rain,' I said.

Cole paid no attention.

'They'll all have Colts,' he said, 'and long guns. There'll be a shotgun, probably Mackie.'

We walked past the stock pens. There was some wind to go with the dark sky. It spun the windmill hard and stirred little dust whirls in front of us as we walked. We stopped at the stock pens. The two stockmen paid us no attention. They kept on talking, staring at the cattle, spitting tobacco juice carefully downwind.

'We come at 'em this way,' Cole said, 'we can

193

keep the cattle between us and them until we're close.'

The wind had picked up. It was whirling the dust now up past eye level, and pushing the tumbleweed along pretty briskly.

'Today be a good day to die?' I said.

'We ain't gonna die,' Cole said.

'Good to know,' I said.

Cole didn't say anything. He was looking at everything, walking through the fight as if he had already seen the rehearsal. He stopped.

'We'll be here when it starts,' he said. 'They'll be there. They'll be spread out. When it happens, I'll look for Ring. You look for Mackie. I don't know how good Russell is, but I do know how good the other two are.'

'Bragg?' I said.

'We shoot him last,' Cole said. 'Bragg's probably a good shooter. Probably killed some people. But I don't know if he can stand his ground.'

'You 'n me are gonna kill four men,' I said.

'If Bragg stands. Otherwise, three.'

'Well, I guess if we don't,' I said, 'we'll never know it.'

'Probably not,' Cole said.

'So I guess it don't matter too much,' I said.

'Probably doesn't,' Cole said.

The wind pushed a tumbleweed past us toward the shed. It bounced a little as it moved across the wagon ruts. I could taste rain on the wind, though none had fallen.

'We'll get to here,' Cole said, 'without nobody's fired, 'cause the cows are in the way. So from here, just past this corner post, we go right at 'em and we go fast. I'll take Ring first, you look for Mackie. And we'll see what develops.'

I looked at the clock on the train station steeple. It read 12:23.

'I could use some coffee,' Cole said.

And we walked back toward the hotel, with the wind whipping around us, trying to take our hats.

CHAPTER 42

Cole and I were drinking coffee at the hotel,
Allie came and sat with us. She didn't
have much to say. She seemed somehow
smaller than she usually was.

'We go up against Russell,' I said to Cole, 'we're
going up against the law in this town.'

'We're the law in our town,' Cole said.

Cole held his coffee cup in both hands, his
elbows on the table.

'Probably deputize Ring and Mackie.'

'Probably,' Cole said.

We were quiet. Cole sipped his coffee, still with
his elbows on the table, still with the cup in both
hands. He didn't look at Allie.

'Makes the law thing a little confusin',' I said.

Cole nodded and didn't answer.

'Guess it's best not to worry about that right
now,' I said.

'He took my prisoner. He broke the law in my
town,' Cole said.

Allie sat very still, like a child allowed to sit with
the adults. Her hands were folded in her lap. She
sat straight in her chair, her feet close together.

The hotelkeeper's wife came and poured us some more. Cole had laid his big pocket watch on the table. It showed one o'clock.

'Aren't either of you afraid?' Allie said.

Cole looked startled.

'Afraid?'

'Yes.' Allie's voice seemed as small as she did. 'Aren't you afraid that you'll be killed?'

Cole frowned a little and stared out past Allie through the hotel door at the street for a little while.

'I don't know, Allie,' he said after a while. 'I been doing this a long time. Maybe I am. But I guess I don't think about it much.'

He looked at me.

'You ever think about it, Everett?'

'Sure.'

'You scared?'

'Sure.'

'Probably a good thing,' Cole said. 'Makes you a little quicker.'

I nodded.

'I'm scared all the time,' Allie said.

'Of what?' Cole said.

'Everything.'

'Like what?'

'Like being alone, or being with the wrong man, having no money, no place to live. If I don't have a man, what am I supposed to do?'

'You got an answer for that, Everett?'

'You could play the piano at the Boston House,' I said.

197

'For the rest of my life?'

'I'll look out for you,' Cole said.

'For how long?'

'Long as you need.'

'Virgil, you could be dead in an hour.'

Cole shook his head.

'Let's go back to Appaloosa right now,' Allie said.

'Got to finish this thing up with Ring Shelton,' Cole said.

'There's four of them.'

Cole shrugged and drank coffee.

'The man who runs the hotel told me that the Shelton brothers were famous gunmen.'

'Got to get things back in balance,' Cole said.

'If you'll take me back to Appaloosa with you, I'll love you all my life. I'll never make you mad. I'll never do anything you don't like.'

'That'll be fine, Allie,' Cole said. 'Soon's Everett and me get things straightened out with Ring.'

'And Mackie,' I said, 'and Russell and Bragg.'

'Sure,' Cole said.

'If they kill you, what'll happen to me?' Allie said.

'Ring'll look out for you,' Cole said.

Allie put her face in her hands and hunched over the table.

'Oh, God,' she said, and began to cry into her hands. 'Oh, my dear God.'

CHAPTER 43

At ten minutes past two o'clock, we went up to our rooms and got ready. I put on a jacket so I could use the pockets. I slipped a five-shot, .32, hammerless pocket pistol in the left-hand pocket. I put twenty eight-gauge shells in the right. I wore a Colt .45 on my gun belt. I checked the load in the shotgun. Cole wore two Colts on belts with cartridge loops. The Colt on his left side was butt-forward. He carried a .45 Winchester. He checked both Colts and made sure there was a round in the chamber of the Winchester. He left the Winchester cocked. It was 2:25. We both put on our hats.

'Remember,' Cole said. 'We walked through this already.'

'It'll be just the same,' I said. ''Cept for them trying to shoot us.'

'I'm hopin' to shoot them first,' Cole said.

'Me, too.'

'But remember,' Cole said. 'Steady's more important than fast.'

'Virgil,' I said, 'you've told me that before every fight we ever had.'

'Anything you want to go over?' Cole said.

'Nope.'

Cole nodded and looked at his watch.

'Don't want to get there too soon,' he said. 'Want to have sort of a flow, you understand, some kind of rhythm, like dancing or something. Just walk down there and arrive on time and start shooting without never breaking stride.'

I nodded like I hadn't heard it before. I could feel the feeling beginning to build. The little hard clutch in my stomach getting tighter, my throat closing so it was hard to swallow. My mouth was dry. I wanted to breathe in more air than I had capacity for. I could feel my heart.

'Okay,' Virgil said. 'Here we go.'

The rain that I had tasted earlier had arrived. It was hard and slanted by the wind. The street was muddy with it. I yanked my hat down tighter.

'Distance we're shooting at,' Cole said, 'wind won't be an issue.'

It was behind us as we walked, which meant at the end of the walk, if it didn't shift, the rain would be blowing at them.

'Won't do no harm to keep an eye out for Bragg,' Cole said. 'I think he'll stick with Ring. I don't think he's got the stuff to go it alone, but if he does, he's a certain sure back shooter.'

We passed the bank. There was no one on the street. Everything was buttoned up against the rain. I thought about Allie's questions.

'You feel it?' I said to Cole.

'Dry mouth? Thing in the stomach? Not enough air?'

'Yeah.'

'Sure, I feel it. You don't feel nothing, there's not much point in doing a thing.'

'You like the feeling?' I said.

Cole didn't speak for so long that I thought he wasn't going to. He, too, had his hat yanked down low over his forehead to keep it on. We slogged through the thickening mud toward the stock pens.

'After,' Cole said.

'And if you didn't have the feeling before, the feeling after wouldn't be so good,' I said.

'I guess,' Cole said.

CHAPTER 44

They were where Cole said they'd be. Four of them, Bragg closest to the shed. The wind was at our backs, blowing the rain hard at them. The steers huddled together in the pens.

'We pass that corner,' Cole said. 'We start shooting and go fast, straight at them.'

I didn't say anything. My mouth was dry. Most of the shootouts we'd been in had sort of erupted, and you didn't have much time to think about it. This one had moved forward for days with the formality of a procession. And now here it was, in the blowing rain.

We turned the corner, and Cole shot Ring Shelton in the chest, and everyone else started shooting at the same time. Something slammed into my left side and tried to knock me down as I cut loose with the eight-gauge. Both barrels. It knocked Mackie Shelton over backward. To my left, Cole was down. Another bullet hit me in my right leg, and I felt it give under me. Cole squirmed sideways in the mud, working the lever on the Winchester. He fired three times, pumping the lever as fast as he fired. Russell staggered and took two steps forward to right himself and raised his Colt and fell face-forward into the mud. I dropped the eight-gauge as I went down and jerked the Colt. Sitting in the mud, I looked for Bragg. He was gone. With Cole on his stomach and me on my backside, we kept our aim on the shed. After a minute or so, we heard the sound of a horse running in the mud, and then, too far to shoot, we saw Bragg ride off.

It was over.

I tried to stand. I couldn't. One shot had broken some ribs on my left side. The other had got me in the top of the right thigh. The thigh was bleeding steadily. The ribs made it painful to move, but I knew I had to cut down on the bleeding. I took my jacket off, and my shirt, and folded the shirt and got the belt off my pants and made a big, clumsy pressure bandage on the thigh.

'Virgil?' I said.

Cole still lay on his stomach in the mud, his rifle cocked, looking at the men strewn in front of us in the mud.

'Both legs,' he said. 'The right one's broke.'

'Took about a minute,' I said.

'Everybody could shoot,' Cole said.

His voice sounded strained. So did mine. The clerk from the train station came out and looked at us from the edge of the station. The two stock-yard hands stood with him. I yelled to them.

'There a doctor in town?'

'Railroad doc,' the clerk shouted. 'Lives at the hotel.'

'Get him,' I said.

Hollering made my ribs hurt. So did breathing. The clerk spoke to one of the stock hands, and he set off at a run toward the hotel. I clenched my teeth and let myself fall backward onto the cold mud. The rain came down cold and steady on my face. I felt hot. I breathed as shallowly as I could.

'Virgil?' I said.

'I'm still here,' Virgil said.

'Well,' I said. 'Doctor'll either save us or he won't.'

And I closed my eyes and let the rain fall on me, and the feel of it began to dwindle and then it was gone and I didn't know anything else.

CHAPTER 45

We gave the horses and the mule to the doctor for his fee. He got us wrapped and bandaged and splinted, and supplied us enough laudanum so we could stand to ride the train to Yaqui and take another one to Appaloosa. We used up most of the laudanum by the time we got there. And when we got off the train in Appaloosa, cooked well done on tincture of opium, Cole on crutches and me with a cane, and Allie fluttering around us, I don't think anyone in Appaloosa felt safer. We was laid up for longer than either of us could stand. Through it, Allie nursed Cole like he was made of hammered gold. And, now and then, she would stop in on me.

While we were gone, Stringer had come down from the sheriff's office to fill in, and he stayed while we recuperated.

Cole was out of pain and could move around on crutches in a few days. There were two ribs broken on my left side, and they took a while. But eventually we were both able to taper off the laudanum and sit outside on the porch at the Boston House and look at whatever was happening in front of us.

It was a hell of a lot more than the Sheltons could do.

Stringer came down from the marshal's office one morning and sat with us for a while.

'Got a posse up and went back to Chester, but we lost your trail once you left that arroyo.'

'Figured you would,' Cole said.

'Get a posse or lose your trail?' Stringer said.

'Both.'

Stringer nodded. He got out a cigar, didn't offer one to either of us, bit off the end, and lit it. When he had it burning right, he leaned back with one foot up on the railing of the porch and his hat tilted forward over his eyes.

'You know you killed a peace officer, duly appointed and sworn,' Stringer said, 'up there in Beauville.'

'Had to,' Cole said.

Stringer watched a woman in a big hat walk along on the shady side of the street. He smiled.

'Sure,' he said.

We all watched the woman as she paused and looked in the window of the dry goods store past the Silver Spur Saloon. After a moment, she went inside.

'You killed all three of 'em,' Stringer said.

'Yep.'

'I knew you were good, Virgil,' Stringer said. 'Everett, too.'

I was an afterthought.

'But I'd a said that nobody could beat the Sheltons, two against three.'

'Four,' I said.

'Oh, yeah,' Stringer said. 'Bragg. What about Bragg?'

'Can't chase him all over the country,' Cole said.

''Course not,' Stringer said. 'Kinda funny, ain't it. You kill three men and get shot half to pieces yourselves to get Bragg back, and you don't get him back.'

'That is funny,' I said. 'If my ribs didn't hurt, I'd be laughing every morning.'

'Ribs take a while,' Stringer said.

It was a bright, warm day with a few small, high, white clouds and a mild breeze that smelled faintly of grass and sage. The lady in the big hat came out of the dry goods store and headed farther up the street. When she reached the corner, she turned and was out of sight.

'Sheriff ain't planning to press matters on you boys about the killings in Beauville, even Russell.'

'You have anything to do with that?' Cole said.

'I tole the sheriff how things were.'

'Kind of you,' Cole said.

Stringer grinned again.

'I didn't want to be the one had to bring you in,' he said.

'Wouldn't be too hard right now,' Cole said.

'Well, it ain't going to be necessary. You boys going to stick around here when you're on your feet?'

I looked at Cole.

'Sure,' he said. 'Got a house here.'

'Gonna move in with Allie?' Stringer said.

'I surely am,' Cole said.

CHAPTER 46

After we healed up, and Cole's house was finished, I went there to eat supper with him and Allie. It was Allie's first time having somebody in to eat, and she had a table-cloth out and a full set of good china with only a couple of pieces that didn't match. We had some soup and some sort of meat pie, and some wine. I didn't like the wine much, but I drank some to be polite. For dessert, there was dried apple pie, which I liked.

'Everett,' Allie said. 'I don't think I've ever said enough to you about how you rescued me from everyone.'

'Virgil did most of that,' I said. 'I just trailed along.'

'You did a lot. I'll never forget you riding out all alone and that Indian coming and touching you and riding off.'

'It didn't do me no harm,' I said. 'And he got to count coup on me and be a hero.'

'I never did understand that,' Allie said. 'What was all that about? Why didn't he try to kill you? Why did they all ride off?'

'He gets close enough to his enemy to touch him, and then ride away, he's a bigger hero than if he killed me,' I said. 'And he didn't just do it with a coup stick. He done it with his hand. And held it on me. And with the other braves watching. Man's a great hero now.'

'And it let 'em off the hook,' Cole said. 'They knew there was six men, with a lot of guns, dug in at a good place to defend, plenty of food and water.'

'So him counting coup on me let them ride off without dishonor,' I said.

'Oh, God,' Allie said. 'Dishonor. Don't seem to make much difference, Indian or white. Men are so silly.'

She shook her head.

'Dishonor!' she said again.

Cole was quiet, sipping his wine. I could tell he didn't like it, either. I didn't know enough about wine to say. But I was pretty sure it wasn't very good wine.

'Well, I just wanted to be sure I said thank you proper.'

'No need,' I said.

'And,' she said. 'I want you to know how embarrassed I am that you saw me . . . you know . . . with Ring Shelton.'

'You did what you had to do,' I said.

Cole seemed mildly interested.

'And I'm mortified,' she said, 'that you saw me with no clothes on.'

Christ!

I looked at Cole. He showed no change of expression.

'Allie,' I said. 'It was a pleasure.'

'Oh, Everett,' she said, and blushed brightly.

Cole smiled a little.

'Well, you started talkin' about it,' he said.

'I know,' Allie said. 'It's just that I'm so grateful. I know that you did it for me. Rode all that way. Went through all that danger. For me.'

'Well, you sure are worth it,' I said.

'Point of fact,' Cole said, 'wasn't just you. We was after Bragg, too.'

'Virgil, I know you killed those men because of me.'

Cole leaned back and looked at me, and then at Allie.

'We did what we needed to do,' he said finally.

'And Everett, too. I will always be grateful to you. You didn't abandon me.'

'No, I didn't,' I said. 'But, you know, I am the deputy city marshal here, and it was sort of what I was hired to do, to find escaped prisoners, to save kidnapped women. That sort of thing.'

'Oh, go ahead,' Allie said, 'the both of you. Be modest. Pretend you were just doing what any lawman would have done. In my heart I know it, and I treasure it. That you did what you did for me.'

Cole looked at me again. But he didn't say anything more. I knew what was bothering him.

211

It was bothering me, too. If Allie was right, and we tracked down the Sheltons and killed them because they had mistreated Cole's girlfriend, then we might be good men. And we might have done the right thing. But we didn't do it as lawmen. And we hadn't done the legal thing.

And where did that leave us?

CHAPTER 47

Two nights later, I lay in bed in my room at the Boston House with Katie Goode, after we'd done our business, and talked about Allie.

'Don't you see what she's doing?' Katie said.

'Being nice to her husband's friend,' I said.

'Husband? They got married?'

'I don't think so. But that's what they call each other.'

Katie shrugged.

'What is it they call it in a war,' she said, 'when a general doesn't use all his troops but holds some out.'

'The troops are in reserve?'

'Yes. That's what I was trying to say. Allie has you in reserve.'

'Reserve? Reserve for what?'

'In case Virgil gets killed.'

'She has me standing by to replace Virgil?'

'Virgil dies, you replace him. Then you're the stud horse. That's why she's so nice to you. That's why there's no more talk of how you molested her that day, at the house before it was finished.'

'Praise be,' I said.

'And she reminded you how you saw her naked.'

'Yeah,' I said, 'she did.'

'That was a kind of flirting, you dumb man.'

'Right in front of Virgil?'

Katie smiled. 'He's a dumb man, too.'

'So why is she so set that everything we did was for her?'

'Oh, Everett,' Katie said. 'You ain't that stupid.'

'I ain't?'

''Course you ain't. Just think a minute.'

I was quiet while I thought about it.

'Makes her feel important,' I said, after a time.

'Um-hm,' Katie said.

'You learn all this stuff being a whore?' I said.

Katie smiled.

'I spend my working time with men,' she said. 'But my social time is with women.'

'All women know things like this?' I said.

'Most of us understand Allie French,' Katie said.

'What do you all understand?'

'She ain't no different,' Katie said, 'from any of us working girls. She's willing to fuck who she got to fuck, so she can get what she needs to get.'

'How 'bout love?' I said. 'Love got anything to do with it?'

'Out here, love's pretty hard for a woman,' Katie said. 'Mostly it's the men worry about love. You know how many miners and cowboys told me they loved me just before they, ah, emptied their chamber?'

'Tell you the truth, Katie,' I said, 'I guess I don't want to know that.'

'Men maybe can worry 'bout love,' Katie said. 'Most women out here got to think 'bout other things.'

'Ever been in love?' I said.

Katie laughed.

'I don't love you, Everett,' she said. 'But you're as close as I come.'

'So what do you feel?'

'I like you,' she said. 'You're not mean. And you got some education. I'm always glad when it's you that hires me, and I'm always glad when you pay for the night.'

'You think that's how Allie feels about Virgil?'

'I don't know what she feels,' Katie said. 'She probably don't know how she feels, either. She just knows he's the top hand, and she'll stay with him till he ain't.'

'Well, what I know is I paid for the night, and I don't want us wasting time.'

'Just passing time while you recovered,' Katie said.

She put her hand under the covers.

'And I do believe you have,' she said.

CHAPTER 48

I had a scar across the top of my right thigh that looked like someone had laid a hot poker on there. But it didn't hurt, and neither did my ribs. Cole was healed up, too, except for a little limp. Stringer went back to Yaqui, and we went back to the marshal's office.

One morning I went out to look at the town, got back to the marshal's office just before lunchtime, and found an aldermen's meeting going on. Cole was at his desk, smoking a cigar. Abner Raines was standing in front of him. Earl May was sitting on the edge of my desk, and Phil Olson was sitting in my chair. I looked at Cole.

'Come in, Everett,' Cole said. 'Aldermen got something to say.'

All three of them looked nervous. I looked at Olson, sitting in my chair. He saw me look at him, and got up quickly and moved over to the wall beside the door, and leaned against it. I sat at my desk and put one foot up on the edge, and then the other, to take off my spurs. May stood and went over to stand beside Olson.

'First of all,' Raines said, 'town's grateful to you, the way you stood up to Bragg.'

'What you hired us for,' Cole said.

'Well, we're not forgetting it,' Raines said. 'You arrested him, got him tried and convicted.'

Nobody said anything. Raines shifted a little on his feet.

'And I know, we know, that when he escaped, you had to go after him.'

Cole looked interested but neutral. I wondered what the *but* would be.

'And certainly you had to rescue Mrs French.'

Cole nodded.

'And we're proud of you, both of you, for that as well. And we're very pleased that you have recovered so well from your wounds.'

'You boys thinking 'bout giving us a medal or something?' Cole said.

They didn't seem too happy, but they all laughed.

'You used to be a soldier boy, Everett,' Cole said. 'You like a nice medal?'

'Had one,' I said. 'Traded it for something in Nogales. Be goddamned, though, if I can recall what.'

'Guess Everett don't endear a medal like me,' Cole said.

No one seemed to know what to say next. It was Olson who finally took the jump.

'Virgil,' he said, 'we all agree with what Abner said, but . . .'

217

There it was.

'. . . things change, and we got to talk about that.'

Cole nodded and looked at me and grinned.

'No medal?' he said.

'Probably not,' I said.

Olson's fair cheeks had become pink.

'We hired you and Everett to protect us from Bragg and his outfit,' Olson said. 'And you done it so good that he's gone, and so is his outfit.'

Cole puffed quietly on his cigar, rolling it in his mouth now and then with his thumb and three fingers, and taking it out occasionally to admire the glowing end of it.

'And I, we, know you had to go off like you did. But it left the town without any peace officer. We had to get hold of the sheriff's office and have them send somebody down, and that was pretty costly.'

'Plus all them bullets we fired off,' Cole said. 'I'll bet they cost a pretty damn penny.'

'I don't mean it that way,' Olson said. 'We don't. But we got to try to run the town businesslike, being as we're the aldermen.'

Cole didn't comment. I folded my hands on my stomach and put my right foot back up against the edge of my desk and rocked my chair back, and looked at the ceiling.

'And you killed a lot of people,' May said.

It was the first sound he'd made since I came in.

'Probably had to do it,' he said. 'But it makes some

of the people in town a little, ah, sort of, ah, uneasy, I guess. One of those men in Beauville was, you know, the town marshal.'

Cole smoked his cigar and made no comment. The aldermen were all silent. Cole and I were silent. The room was full of silence. Once again, it was Olson who spoke.

'We were wondering if maybe we don't need two men in the marshal's office,' he said.

'Both or none,' Cole said.

'We was thinking maybe you'd want to make more money, now that you and Allie have moved in. We was thinking of offering the job to Everett.'

'Both or none,' I said.

Olson buckled.

'Sure,' he said. 'I understand. No offense. We'll go back home and think on it a little.'

Cole didn't say anything. The aldermen looked at each other.

'Well, we appreciate everything you boys done,' Raines said. 'Just want to be sure you know that.'

The aldermen turned to go.

'You boys sure Bragg won't come back?' I said.

None of them answered. And the subject didn't come up again.

CHAPTER 49

Allie and Cole and I rode up into the hills in back of Bragg's old place, to look for the Appaloosa.

'I want Allie to see him,' Cole said.

'I don't know why, Everett,' Allie said. 'It's not like I've never seen a stallion.'

'That's for certain,' I said.

Cole grinned. Allie lowered her eyes.

'Everett, don't you talk to me like I'm one of your night-time ladies.'

'Hell, Allie, I was just speakin' well of Virgil.'

Bragg's ranch was empty. No stock. No hands. No cook smoke. Stock probably got sold off to pay the Sheltons. Hands had drifted. Things that had started here had gotten people killed. It was sort of hard to remember what they were and how it had spun out. Time had passed. Grass had grown in the empty corral. Some weeds pushed up between the boards on the front porch of the house. The Sheltons were in the ground. Bragg hadn't been heard from. Cole still had a slight limp, but everything else had healed over.

'Been a while,' I said to Cole.

He nodded.

'Do you think we'll see the horse soon?' Allie said.

'Soon,' Cole said.

We rode up the next hillside above the ranch, slow, so Allie wouldn't have trouble staying with us. At the top, we sat our horses and looked west. He was there, not very far from where we'd seen him last. He was moving his mares along the crest of the hill, his ears pricked forward, head tossing, sniffing the air. He was keeping his mares in a tight herd, moving around them, nipping at their flanks to keep them close. Occasionally, he would stop and turn and look around him, his head up, trying to find a scent.

'Something's goin' on,' Cole said.

'Why does he keep biting the mares?' Allie said.

'He wants them close together,' Cole said.

'Why?'

'Cougar maybe,' I said.

'Another stallion,' Cole said.

'You're sure?' Allie said.

'Yes.'

'How can you be so sure?' Allie said.

Cole shrugged.

'It's another stallion,' he said.

And it was. Big. Chestnut-colored. On the side of the hill, moving toward the herd.

'You knew,' Allie said to Cole.

'I did,' Cole said.

'How?'

Cole shrugged again.

'Virgil knows things,' I said.

The chestnut got closer to the running herd. He was running free. The Appaloosa had to herd his mares, and it slowed him. Then the Appaloosa stopped and turned and made a snarling bugle sound at the chestnut. The mares stopped running and gathered. The chestnut reared and bugled back at the Appaloosa. Then they both stood motionless for a moment, looking at each other. The mares stayed close together. The chestnut swished his tail and pulled his lips back from his teeth, and squealed. The Appaloosa exploded. He came at the chestnut with is neck straight out, biting at him. The chestnut bit him back. The Appaloosa reared and slashed at him with his front hooves. The chestnut went up, and they grappled like that, screaming. Then they separated and stood again. There was blood on both of them. The chestnut moved sideways. The Appaloosa moved with him, staying always between him and the mares. The chestnut tried to move around him, and the Appaloosa drove into him again.

'Oh my God,' Allie said. 'Oh my God.'

Our horses, all three of them geldings, stirred uneasily as the two stallions screamed and bit and kicked.

'Oh my God,' Allie said again.

She covered her ears with her hands.

The chestnut made one final attempt to circle around the Appaloosa and get past him to the mares. Then he shied away. The Appaloosa pressed him, and the chestnut shied, kicked with his hind hooves at the Appaloosa, and ran. The Appaloosa went after him, biting at his haunches as he ran. The chestnut went up the next hill and over it. The Appaloosa followed him to the top and stopped. He wouldn't lose sight of the mares. He stood on the hilltop, watching as the chestnut ran off, glancing back every few seconds at the mares.

Allie took her hands from her ears.

'Is it over?' she said.

'Yes,' Cole said.

'That was all about the mares?'

'Yes.'

'Do they always do that?'

'Yes.'

'Why?'

'Stallion wants mares, he's got to fight another stallion.'

'Why does this stallion care if another stallion mounts one of those mares?'

'Ask him,' Cole said.

'But, I mean, it's not love.'

'Probably not,' Cole said.

The Appaloosa pranced back to his mares with his neck arched and his tail high. He was still churning with nervous energy. The mares began to graze as he moved restlessly around the perimeter of their grazing.

'Or jealousy,' Allie said. 'I mean, he's just a damned horse.'

'Them mares,' Cole said, 'belong to that appaloosa stud, long as he's enough horse to keep them. That matters to him, I guess.'

'And what about the mares,' Allie said. 'Do they have any choice?'

'Horses do what they need to do,' Cole said. 'Everett, you been to the United States Military Academy. You know why the mares stay with the stallions?'

'Nope,' I said. 'Mares and stallions probably don't know, either.'

'Horses ain't too smart,' Cole said.

CHAPTER 50

Bragg showed up in the spring. He walked into the city marshal's office in the mid-afternoon of a rainy April day, wearing a rain slicker and, under it, a suit like a banker.

'I'm going to take a piece of paper out of my coat pocket,' he said.

I took my gun out and rested the barrel against the edge of the desk. Bragg took a presidential pardon from an inside pocket and put it on the desk in front of me.

'Absolved of all charges,' Bragg said.

I picked up the document and looked at it for a while. There was a lot of lawyer language, but there was the phrase *absolved of all charges outstanding*, right in the first paragraph. I handed the document back to Bragg.

'You must have come into money,' I said.

'Where's Cole?' Bragg said.

'Out walkin' the town,' I said. 'He'll be back in a while.'

'I'll wait.'

'Not in here,' I said.

'Why not?'

'I don't like you.'

'I don't want Cole to see me and start shooting,' Bragg said, "fore he reads my pardon.'

'Ain't Virgil's style,' I said, and went to the door and held it open.

Bragg hesitated. Then he shook his head and walked outside and sat on one of the chairs in front of the office, under the overhang. I left the door open and went back to my desk, and watched the rain puddle in the street outside.

It was maybe an hour and a half later when Cole came back. I knew he'd have seen Bragg from a long way up the street. And I knew he wouldn't have shown any response. I saw him pass in front of the window. His slicker was unbuttoned so he could get at his gun if he needed to. His collar was turned up against the rain, and his hat was tilted down over his eyes. I stood and went to the door. Cole had stopped in front of Bragg and was looking at him without expression. Bragg had his coat open.

'I'm not heeled,' he said.

Cole nodded. Bragg held up the paper he'd already shown me. I knew it wouldn't mean anything to Cole. He'd have to read it slowly when he had time to make out all the words.

'I been pardoned,' Bragg said. 'I already shown it to Hitch.'

I stepped out and sat down in the chair beside Bragg. Cole glanced at me. I nodded. He looked back at Bragg.

'You was the only one to run off,' Cole said, 'up in Beauville.'

'The ones that stayed are dead,' Bragg said.

Cole didn't speak.

'I'm a law-abiding citizen,' Bragg said. 'You got no call to bother me further.'

Cole was silent for a time, looking at Bragg with no expression.

Finally he said, 'Not 'less you give me cause.'

Bragg smiled widely.

'That's very fine,' he said. 'I'm coming back to Appaloosa. I needed to clear things up with you first.'

Cole didn't answer.

Bragg took a tan leather cigar case out of his inside coat pocket. He offered a cigar to Bragg and to me. We declined. He took one out for himself and got it lit and puffed on it till it was going good.

'I come into some money,' Bragg said, 'and I got plans for coming into more.'

Bragg put out his hand.

'Bygones be bygones?' he said.

Cole ignored him and walked past him into the office. Bragg watched him for a moment. Then he looked at me.

'I'm the right side to be on,' Bragg said. 'I'm going to do some things in Appaloosa.'

I shook my head.

Now that he'd been reassured that Cole wouldn't shoot him dead, Bragg seemed pretty full of himself. He wasn't a dangerous rancher with a fast gun who hired fast gun hands. Now he was a man of means and position. He looked and talked like a politician. He offered cigars and talked of big plans. He wore a suit with a vest. I didn't like this Bragg any better than the other one.

'I won't shake your hand, either,' I said.

Bragg stood and buttoned up his raincoat.

'Things are likely to change in Appaloosa,' Bragg said. 'You could benefit from the changes, or you could get left behind.'

He turned up his collar and adjusted his hat and stepped off the front porch into the rain. I watched him as he walked on down the street, trailing the smell of a pretty good cigar behind him.

CHAPTER 51

It wasn't until the middle of May that I rode up in the early morning to take a look-see at Bragg's ranch. I could smell the smoke and bacon smell from the cookshack long before I topped the rise and looked down at the place. There were horses in the corral and, as best I could make out, more in the barn. The weeds were gone from the front porch. The place looked somehow clean and busy, although I only saw two hands loafing by the corral, where they had slung their saddles on the top rail. Between the ones in the barn and those in the corral, there were horses for a considerable number of hands. I saw no sign of cattle. The two boys leaning on the fence weren't dressed for cattle work. I sat my horse for a time, looking down. Some other hands came and went: to and from the privy, in and out of the bunkhouse, back and forth to the cookshack. None of them seemed dressed for herding cows. I got bored looking at them, so I turned my horse and rode back to town.

Cole was drinking coffee in the Boston House Saloon and studying an illustrated book about

King Arthur. I stopped for a minute and watched him. He read slowly, like he always did, sometimes forming words silently with his lips, sometimes running his forefinger along under an especially hard sentence.

Without looking up he said, 'Come on and set, Everett.'

I did. Tilda came and gave me coffee.

'Bragg's back into his ranch,' I said.

Cole put the book aside.

'I know.'

'Got quite a number of hands,' I said.

'And no cows,' Cole said.

'You been up there, too,' I said.

''Course I have.'

'What do you think is happening?'

'I know he bought both of Earl May's saloons.'

'Really?' I said. 'What's Earl going to do.'

'Says he's going to retire, go live with his daughter in Denver.'

'Maybe we should do that,' I said.

'You got a daughter someplace?' Cole said.

'No.'

'Me, either.'

'Might as well stay here then,' I said. 'Where you suppose Bragg's getting this money?'

'Heard different things,' Cole said. 'Fella told me Bragg had a big silver strike in Nevada. 'Nother fella told me that Bragg and some other boys robbed a train in Mexico that was carrying gold.'

'I heard he was down along the Rio Grande with

some fellas, stealing cows and horses from Mexico,' I said. 'Bringing them back here and selling them to the Army.'

'Hard to get rich doing that,' Cole said.

'But easy to get killed.'

Cole nodded.

'Doesn't sound like Bragg,' he said.

'Hard work, too,' I said.

Cole grinned.

'Doesn't sound like Bragg,' he said.

'I heard he won a pile of nuggets from some drunken miner in a poker game in Abilene,' I said. 'And I heard he took a fortune off a Wells Fargo stage in Clovis.'

Tilda came by and filled our coffee cups. Cole drank some. Then he grinned.

'Maybe he worked hard and honest for it,' Cole said.

'That's probably it,' I said.

'What we do know,' Cole said, 'is he's got a big payroll up at that ranch for a lot of riders that so far's I can see, don't do nothing.'

'And he bought two saloons,' I said. 'Earl get a good price?'

'Seemed happy with it.'

'Any chance Bragg run him off?'

'Don't think so,' Cole said. 'You might ask him.'

'Sure,' I said. 'Why do you think he came back here?'

'Got land here,' Cole said.

'Easy enough to sell.'

'He's got us here, too,' Cole said.

'Think it's got something to do with us?'

'Might. Bragg was the big dog 'round here till we showed up.'

'You think it's got something to do with pride?'

'Pride's a funny thing,' Cole said.

I drank some more coffee and looked at Cole for a time.

'How would you know that?' I said.

CHAPTER 52

Appaloosa had two town meetings every year: one on the first of June, before it got too hot to have a meeting, the other on the first of December, before the real winter hit. The meetings took place in the church at the end of Second Street. They usually lasted all day, and me or Cole always went, to see to it there was no fistfights broke out over ticklish points.

I was there for the June meeting, in the back of the church, by the door, sitting on a saloon lookout chair that was brought in special for the meeting. The aldermen sat in a row up front, beside the pulpit where the pastor stood, moderating the meeting. As always, after the lunch break there was a clean smell of whiskey in the room. While the latecomers were sitting down, Randall Bragg came in and walked alone down the center aisle and sat in the front row. He was dressed in a dark suit. He had a gold watch chain across his vest. He took his hat off as he came into the church and placed it carefully in his lap when he sat down.

Nobody had a gavel in town, so when it was

time for the meeting to start for the afternoon, the pastor came out and stood silently at the pulpit until things got quiet. I was always surprised that it worked. But it always did.

'Before we begin this afternoon's session,' the pastor said, 'we have had a special request from a member of the community to address the members of the meeting.'

The pastor was a strapping man who obviously considered himself a sure bet for heaven.

'With the concurrence of our Board of Aldermen,' the pastor said, 'I have agreed to the request. Mr Bragg?'

Bragg stood, laid his hat on his chair, and stepped to the pulpit. He was clean-shaven, freshly barbered, and, probably, if the room smelled less of whiskey, he would have smelled of bay rum. He glanced toward the ceiling for a moment and then turned to the audience.

'I was fearing maybe there'd be a lightning bolt when I stepped to the pulpit,' he said.

The audience laughed politely.

'And if the Lord has chosen to send one,' Bragg said, 'who could have blamed him.'

The audience laughed again. Bragg smiled at them.

'Most of you know who I am,' he said. 'My name is Randall Bragg, and I have been an evil man for some years.'

Everyone got very quiet.

'A year or so ago, I faced death several times

234

and escaped with my life. It made me wonder why. Why did I not die when so many others had?'

My answer was that in at least one instance, it was because he turned and ran. But I kept my answer to myself.

'It came to me one day like the sun coming through a cloud, that the answer lay in a higher power. God had plans for me. He wanted me to come back to where I'd done so much that was bad, and try to do some good.'

You couldn't even hear people breathing in the room. The big preacher stood beside Bragg, beaming with pride.

'And,' Bragg said, and bowed his head as he said it, 'here I am.'

A sort of long sigh ran through the crowd.

'I've been blessed,' Bragg said. 'In this last year, I've come into money, and I'm back here to use that money, to build this town, where only a short while ago I did so much harm.'

There was a little scattered clapping. Bragg put his hands out to ask for quiet.

'I've bought some property in town, from Earl May,' Bragg said. 'And I'm fixing to renovate it, and today I'd like to tell you all that I've bought the Boston House from Abner Raines.'

A lot of the audience whispered to each other.

'I'm going to turn it into the finest hotel between Saint Louis and Denver,' he said, 'and, with God's help, I'll make Appaloosa into the finest, richest town between the Rockies and the Mississippi

River. It'll be a town where people will come to spend money. It'll be a town where a man, any man willing to work, can be not just well off, he can be rich.'

When Bragg started talking about God's help, I wondered about a thunderbolt myself. But none came. Instead, the audience began to clap and somebody stood up and cheered, and then everyone was on their feet, clapping and cheering. Bragg stood silently, his head bowed reverently, his hands clasped in front of him, and accepted the clapping and cheering modestly and gratefully.

He didn't make clear exactly how he was going to accomplish all this, but nobody seemed to notice. They all liked the idea of working hard and getting rich. Bragg raised his eyes as the applause began to quiet.

'To any here whom I have ever offended, I beg you to forgive me. To all of you here, I thank you for having me back.'

Then he lowered his eyes again, and with his hands still clasped in front of him like some kind of friar, he walked down the aisle of the church to the door. He looked up a little bit as he passed me and nodded and smiled.

It was a hell of a performance.

CHAPTER 53

The bull showed up in a boxcar in the dead heat of July. Two of Bragg's hands met him at the train and began to haze him slowly though town on his way to the ranch. He was a squat, compact bull with a black coat and no horns.

'Ever see one looked like that?' I said to Cole as they moved the bull up Main Street.

'Nope.'

A few boys followed along, looking at the black bull. Some men came to the doors of shops. People stood in the doorway of Bragg's two saloons to look.

'Olson told me Bragg bought it in Scotland. It's a Black Angus.'

'Olson seems pretty snug with Bragg,' Cole said, 'don't he.'

'Olson says Bragg's fixing to start a herd, got some Angus cows coming, too.'

'Sort of small bull,' Cole said.

'Olson says the steers make real good eating,' I said. 'Says that some of the fancy hotels and restaurants back east will pay a lot more for them.'

The hands turned the bull at the foot of the street, and we couldn't see him anymore. The boys trailed around the corner after them.

'Bragg's busy,' Cole said.

'Fancy cows,' I said. 'Saloons, hotels.'

'I hear Abner Raines left town,' Cole said.

'Going where?'

'I think back to Kansas, said he was going to farm a little.'

'Farm?'

'What he said.'

'Who's running the hotel?'

'Bragg put a man in here,' Cole said.

'Be interesting to know where Bragg got his money,' I said.

'That ain't as interesting as what he's gonna do with it,' Cole said.

'You're right,' I said. 'Fact is, where he got it don't matter much.'

Cole nodded.

We were quiet. From where we sat, we could see the bull again, small in the distance, kicking up some dust, going up the hill toward Bragg's ranch.

'So that leaves Olson as the only alderman,' I said.

'Un-huh.'

'And he's getting friendlier with Bragg every day.'

'Un-huh.'

'Next June first,' Cole said, 'town meeting's gonna have to elect some new alderman in October.'

'Gives Bragg 'bout three months,' I said.

'Yep.'

'You think Bragg's really a changed man?' I said.

''Course not.'

'Me, either,' I said. 'What do you think he wants?'

'I think he wants to own this town,' Cole said, 'and everybody in it.'

'And then what?'

'I don't know,' Cole said. 'He probably don't know, either.'

'Well,' I said. 'So far, he ain't buttin' heads with you and me. Like he done last time.'

'Not yet.'

'So there's nothing for us to do about him,' I said.

'Ain't done nothing ain't legal,' Cole said.

'But we know he's going to.'

'We got to wait till he does,' Cole said.

'We know he killed Jack Bell and a deputy.'

Cole nodded.

'We know he hired Ring and Mackie to bust him loose.'

Cole nodded.

'We know Allie got kidnapped in the process.'

'He's been pardoned,' Cole said.

'Not by us,' I said.

'We can't be starting things like that,' Cole said, 'Only way to stay clean is to stay with the rules.'

It was an old discussion. We'd had it before. The outcome never changed.

'Well,' I said after a while, 'he seems to be going at it smarter, this time.'

'He's got some money this time.'

'Money makes it easier to be smart,' I said.

'Never had none,' Cole said. 'So I wouldn't know.'

'I guess I ain't, either,' I said. 'So I guess I don't know. But it seems like it would be easier.'

'Might be harder,' Cole said.

'Might be, I suppose. When you think of it, there ain't that much a fella needs.'

'If he lives alone,' Cole said.

'If he lives alone,' I said.

'Allie likes things,' Cole said.

'She plays the piano. She gets paid,' I said. 'And tips.'

'She wants more.'

'Got a nice house,' I said.

Cole didn't say anything for a while.

'Always had enough,' Cole said.

I nodded.

'You got enough,' Cole said.

'I do,' I said. 'I got a place to sleep. I can buy whiskey and food and feed the horse and purchase a pump from Katie Goode when I need one. I get cigars from you once in a while. I had more money, I don't know what I'd do with it.'

'You could give it to Allie,' Cole said. 'She'd know.'

I grinned.

'She wants me to get another job.'

'You want to do that?'

'I'm good at this,' Cole said.

Barely visible now, the black bull disappeared over the crest of the far hill. The hint of dust hung for a minute where the bull had gone, and then it dispersed and nothing moved on the hilltop.

'You are,' I said.

CHAPTER 54

We had a miner in jail for beating up a whore named Big Ass Sally Lowe, and I had sat and listened to him all day. Now it was Cole's turn, and I went up to the Boston House Saloon for supper and a drink.

The saloon at the Boston House was looking good. There was a big, new, dark mahogany bar, and a big, new, gilt-trimmed mirror behind it, and a big chandelier with a lot of cut glass in the middle of the room. There were four card tables in the back and a man to deal faro. Bragg had made a deal with Phil Olson, the lone remaining alderman, for a special deputy with powers limited to the hotel, who sat lookout with a shotgun in a high chair near the faro layout.

Allie had a new piano to play, which was a waste of money, and she was playing hard when I sat down near the bar. Bragg was there, dark suit, white shirt, gold chain, good cigar. He came to my table.

'Buy you a drink, Everett?'

'Got one,' I said.

Bragg turned his palms up.

'Fine,' he said. 'Perfectly fine. Cigar?'

I shook my head.

'Fine,' he said again. 'I understand why you boys are feeling hard about me. But I want you to know I ain't the man I was, and I'm hopin' we can work together once you boys come to see the truth of my statement.'

'That statement being that you're a reformed man.'

'I am.'

'Who now owns two saloons, a hotel, and an expensive black bull,' I said.

'And six heifers,' Bragg said and smiled. 'I'm going to raise beef that most folks have never tasted, and, when they do, they won't be able to get enough of it.'

'With a bull and six cows.'

'My cows are just the start. I'm arranging for some other folks to start ranching Angus heifers, and my bull will do the service.'

'I thought you was already rich,' I said.

'I had some good luck,' Bragg said. 'Now I want to give this town good luck, make up for all the bad luck I brought it in the past.'

'You're going to bring us luck?' I said.

'I'm going to make Appaloosa famous for its beef. I want to develop the copper mines properly. It's going to be a place where people want to come, where people can have a good time, where people will want to invest money.'

I sipped some whiskey and leaned my chair onto

its back legs and put one foot against the edge of the table and teetered a little.

'Bragg,' I said. 'Let's you and me understand each other. I don't believe a single fucking word you say. You want to turn Appaloosa into your private town, and you're working your ugly ass off to get on the good side of Virgil and me, so we won't stop you.'

I took another sip.

'Which we will,' I said.

Something moved just for a second behind Bragg's face, then it was gone. When he spoke, his voice was the same jolly voice he was using these days.

'Sorry to hear you say that, Everett. I was hoping I could work with you and Virgil.'

I didn't answer him.

'Well,' he said with his big friendly smile. 'Time will tell.'

I didn't say anything, and Bragg walked over to the piano where Allie was playing 'My Old Kentucky Home.' I think.

'You know 'Old Folks at Home,' Allie?' Bragg said.

'Of course I do, Mr Bragg.'

'Please call me Randall,' Bragg said. 'Always did love that song.'

Allie began to play the tune, and Bragg stood listening, as if the song had captured him. To me, it didn't sound too much different than 'My Old Kentucky Home.'

'You like Stephen Foster, Randall?'

'I do.'

'I love him, too,' Allie said.

Bragg went to the bar and got a drink and brought it back and put it on top of the piano.

'I haven't really had much chance to talk with you since the Indians almost got us.'

Allie nodded.

'I just wanted to tell you I admired your courage.'

'Oh, bless my soul, Randall, I was terrified.'

'Well, I thought you were very brave.'

He drank some of his drink.

'Could I buy you a small glass of something? We have sherry now, you know.'

'A glass of sherry would be lovely,' Allie said.

There was a sound in her voice I'd heard before. It wasn't a good sound. Bragg went and got her a glass of sherry and brought it back. She sipped a little and put it down on the piano and began to play 'Camptown Races.' Bragg leaned against the piano, listening, as if it was good.

Without looking up, Allie said, 'I'm always embarrassed when anyone talks about that. I mean, Randall, you saw me all undressed.'

'I don't mean to be forward, Allie,' Bragg said. 'But I remember that moment happily.'

Allie giggled.

'Randall, you are making me blush,' she said.

Bragg laughed.

'Nothin' to be ashamed of, Allie. Fact is, as I recall, there's a lot to be proud of.'

'Oh, my,' Allie said.

I got up and walked over and leaned my fore-arms on the piano and didn't say anything. Allie kept playing.

'We were just talking about that terrible time with the Indians,' Allie said.

'I heard,' I said.

'Randall just bought me a lovely glass of sherry, Everett,' Allie said.

I nodded. Bragg didn't say anything. Allie begin to play 'Oh! Susanna.' Bragg and I stood and listened.

When Allie finished, Bragg said, 'Thank you for the nice recital, Allie.'

'Thank *you*, Randall,' Allie said. 'For the sherry.'

Bragg nodded and walked away. I stayed. I was trying to think of what I wanted to say.

'Have to be nice to him, Everett,' Allie said. 'Since he bought the hotel, he's my boss.'

I nodded, took another drink of whiskey, and walked away. I knew what it was I wanted to say, but I knew there wasn't a way to say it, and even if there was, it wouldn't do no good.

CHAPTER 55

Bragg had a good summer. He and some investors in Denver bought up the two copper mines, which had created Appaloosa in the first place, and began to rework them. The hotel was always full now, and the saloons. The gambling operations were expanding, and each one had a special deputy in the lookout chair. In late August, Bragg bought out Olson and added the livery stable and a general store to his holdings. His heifers were pregnant.

It was late in the day in the middle of September and rainy when a slim man with a young, smooth face came into the marshal's office where Cole and I were drinking coffee and watching the rain through the open door. He was wearing a slicker unbuttoned and I could see that he had a .44 Colt with a pearl handle under it.

Cole looked at him carefully for a moment.

'Hayes,' he said.

'Hello, Virgil,' the man said.

He took his hat off and slapped it against his leg to shake off some of the rain, and put the hat on the edge of Cole's desk. His hair was gray. Taking his hat off aged him.

'My deputy,' Cole said, nodding at me, 'Everett Hitch. Hayes Hatfield.'

We said hello.

'Heard about you boys and the Sheltons,' Hatfield said.

''Gainst city regulations,' Cole said, 'to be carrying a gun in town.'

'Always is in your towns, Virgil. I figured you'd give a little slack on that.'

Cole nodded.

'I will,' Cole said. 'How long you in town.'

'Be gone tomorrow,' Hatfield said.

'Appreciate you didn't stroll around with the gun showing,' Cole said. 'Sorta undercuts the law.'

'I'll keep my coat closed,' Hatfield said.

'But not buttoned,' Cole said.

'Gun don't do you much good buttoned up under your coat,' Hatfield said.

'No,' Cole said. 'It don't.'

'Mostly I'm just going to get some supper and go to sleep,' Hatfield said.

'You got business in Appaloosa?' Cole said.

Hatfield smiled a wide smile. Except for the gray hair, he looked about twenty.

'Fella came over to Yaqui to see me. I'm dealing cards there, in the Crystal Palace, doing a little work for Wells Fargo. He said he was going to be

248

the first mayor in Appaloosa, and he wondered if I might like to be the city marshal.'

'Didn't know the job was open,' Cole said.

'Said it was gonna be, soon as he was mayor.'

Cole didn't say anything.

'Said the town was growing so fast that they'd be organizing a police department, and as soon as they did, I'd be the chief.'

'Hadn't heard that,' Cole said.

'So I asked around a little,' Hatfield said, 'and I found out that you was the marshal here, and I thought I might come over here and talk to you about it.'

'Who was the fella you talked to,' Cole said.

'Fella named Olson,' Hatfield said.

Cole looked at me.

'So he's in with Bragg,' he said.

'In deep,' I said.

'Bragg the fella you didn't kill up in Beauville?'

'He run,' Cole said.

'And he come back?' Hatfield said.

'He come back with money,' I said. 'Bought out most of the town.'

'You boys stopping him from buying all of it?'

'Yes.'

'He don't dare go up against you straight on,' Hatfield said.

'Don't seem to,' Cole said.

'And he thinks I would,' Hatfield said.

'You would,' Cole said, 'if there was reason.'

'And if I hired on with this Olson fella . . .'

'There'd be reason,' Cole said.

Hatfield picked his hat up off the corner of the desk and held it against his left thigh while he stood in the doorway for a moment and watched it rain.

'Rainy fall,' he said.

'Startin' out that way,' Cole said.

Hatfield put his hat on and adjusted it so that it tilted a little forward over his eyes.

'Sounds to me a fella took this job, he might be working for Bragg.'

'That would be correct,' Cole said. 'Olson's just the errand boy.'

Hatfield nodded, his back to us, still looking at the rain through the open door. Then he turned and looked around the little marshal's office.

'Don't seem like a place I'd care to work,' he said.

Virgil and I both nodded.

'If I was here,' Hatfield said, 'wouldn't let him run me off.'

'I got a house here,' Cole said. 'And a woman.'

'Even if you didn't. You wouldn't let him run you off.'

'No,' Cole said, 'I guess I wouldn't.'

'However,' Hatfield said. 'Since I ain't here, I don't see no reason to come here.'

'Correct,' Cole said.

Hatfield turned back from the door and put his hand out. Cole shook it. Then I did.

'I'll be on the train back to Yaqui tomorrow,' Hatfield said.

Then he turned and walked out the open door, holding his coat closed, and walked toward the Boston House.

CHAPTER 56

It was chilly and still raining when I walked down to the marshal's office in the morning. Cole was sitting outside under the overhang, out of the rain. It didn't seem like good sitting-out weather.

I said, 'Morning, Virgil.'

Cole nodded, and I went in and got some coffee off the stove and poured it and brought it out, and sat in the other chair. Cole didn't say anything. He didn't seem to be looking at anything or thinking about anything. He seemed to be just sitting. I sat with him and drank some coffee. It had been raining three days now. Main Street was a slough of mud. A few saddle horses moved heavily through it, but there was no wagon traffic.

'They ain't going to run me off,' Cole said.

'We got hired,' I said. 'We can get fired.'

'Me and Allie got a house here. I'm staying.'

'What you gonna stay as?' I said.

'Ain't got to that yet,' Cole said.

'They ain't gonna pay us,' I said.

'I know,' Cole said.

I drank some coffee.

'Might make some sense to move on,' I said.

Cole shook his head.

'You talk this over with Allie?' I said.

Cole nodded.

'She won't go,' I said.

'No.'

I closed my eyes for a minute and opened them slowly and looked at the rain some more.

'And you won't go without her.'

'No.'

The wet smell was strong. Wet wood, wet mud, wet horses. It mixed with the smell of wood smoke as people fired up stoves against the first rainy chill of early fall. I took in some air and let it out slowly.

So here we are.

'I got to say some things, Virgil.'

Cole nodded.

'I stay here,' he said, 'and I won't be able to make a living.'

'Soon as Olson's mayor, he'll fire us, and no one else will hire us.'

'I know,' Cole said.

He was still motionless. Looking at nothing. Thinking of nothing. Being nothing.

'I got something else,' I said.

'She might leave me,' Cole said.

A rider went by on a small sorrel horse. I watched the rain puddle in the collapsing imprint of the horse's hooves. I took in another long breath and tightened my stomach muscles and hunched my shoulders and said it.

253

'She will,' I said. 'You saw how it was with Ring Shelton. Once you ain't the stud horse anymore . . .'

Cole tipped his chair back further and looked up at the sky with his head resting against the weathered exterior of the office wall.

'I won't leave her,' he said.

CHAPTER 57

It was mid-afternoon the second Monday in October. Cole had taken a prisoner to Yaqui and would be back Wednesday, which left the town for me to police.

It was brisk as I walked the town. When the sun went down, it would be cold. I went into the saloon at the Boston House to warm up and get some coffee. The room was quiet and noisy. Allie was playing the piano, adding to the noise. I got some coffee and stood at the bar to drink it. I saw Bragg come into the saloon through the lobby entrance. He bought a bottle of brandy at the far end of the bar, then walked to Allie and whispered to her. She put her head back and laughed. He whispered something else, and she nodded. Then he left and went back out through the lobby door.

Allie played two more songs, then stood, lowered the keyboard lid, and walked out toward the lobby. After a moment, I put my cup down and walked out after her. She wasn't there.

'Mrs French pass by here?' I said.

The clerk nodded toward the stairs.

'She went up,' he said.

I nodded.

'Bragg keep a room here?'

'I'm not supposed to tell, Everett.'

'Peter,' I said. 'I am the damned law, remember?'

'Two-oh-five,' he said.

'Thank you.'

I went outside and stood on the porch for a time and breathed the clean, cold air. Then I turned back into the lobby and went past the clerk and up the stairs to the second floor. It was quiet. I walked the length of it without hearing anything interesting. So I settled my back against the wall beside the window at the far end of the hall and waited. The late-afternoon sun slanted past me down the hall. I could see the little dust particles floating in it.

I wasn't happy. I knew what I was going to find out. I was there in part, I guess, because I kept hoping I wouldn't find it out. That there'd be nothing to find out. I knew better, but knowing and wanting ain't always the same. And when I found out, then what was I going to do? I didn't have to decide that until I found it out. I tried to keep my mind blank as I stood and waited.

The sun was a lot lower when the door opened to room 205 and Allie walked out. Bragg stood behind her in the doorway and she turned to kiss him one more time. It was a hard, hot kiss, and it lasted awhile. I stood where I was, feeling sort of sick. When the kiss ended, she pulled away from him, and they both saw me standing down the hall. She flinched. Bragg stepped back into the room and closed the door. In the silent hall, I could hear the bolt slide. Allie stared at me. I looked back. Then she gave me an odd, nasty smile and tossed her head a little and flounced away. I stood for a time where I was in the empty hall. I could kick Bragg's door in. But then what? I could confront Allie. But then what? Cole would be back from Yaqui in the morning. And, good Jesus Christ, then what?

CHAPTER 58

Cole was a half hour off the night train ride back from Yaqui. Allie wasn't home. He and I were eating a late breakfast at Café? Paris. Actually, for Cole it was a late breakfast. For me it was a second. But that was okay. I liked breakfast.

'How'd you get into this work, Virgil?' I said.

'I was always good with a gun,' Cole said. 'I guess I practiced some, but most of it sort of came natural.'

'You ever kill a man not legal?' I said.

'Meaning what?' Cole said.

'You ever shoot a man because he done you wrong? Or you didn't like him? Or he made you mad?'

'Depends what you mean by legal,' Cole said. 'First time was self-defense. Fella started up with me in a bar in Las Cruces. He wanted to take it outside, so we did, and I killed him.'

He smiled.

'It's how I started,' he said. 'Marshal offered me a job.'

'Did it bother you?'

'The first time,' Cole said. 'No. You?'

'Nope,' I said. 'Ever bother you since?'

'I knew right off, when I took to marshaling, that there needed to be rules. I never killed nobody outside the rules.'

'Never?'

'Nope. I would arrest anyone broke the law. If they wouldn't submit to arrest, I'd kill them, but I never killed them first.'

'Sometimes,' I said, 'you probably knew they wouldn't submit.'

'That would be their choice,' Cole said.

'Even though you might have pushed them into a corner?'

'They always had the chance to be arrested and go to jail,' Cole said. 'You know that, Everett. What the hell are we talking about?'

'Just thinking about it,' I said.

'Don't think about it too much,' Cole said. 'Keep it simple. You represent the law.'

'Even if it's law you wrote up.'

'As long as it's the law,' Cole said. 'And you stand by it.'

I nodded.

'Otherwise, what the hell are you?' I said.

'Otherwise, you're Ring Shelton,' Cole said.

'His word was good,' I said.

'It was,' Cole said. 'And he wasn't a back shooter. But he weren't a lawman. He'd kill anybody, long as somebody hired him to do it.'

'Maybe that was his law,' I said.

Cole gestured the Chinaboy for more coffee.

'Ain't enough,' Cole said.

'I always kind of figured boys like you and me, Virgil, we done gun work because we could. We was better at it than most, and we didn't mind. It's better than punching cows, or digging copper, or soldiering. And if you do it as a peace officer, you get paid regular, and you sort of know when to do it and how.'

'Sounds right,' Cole said.

'But I never took the legal stuff too serious. It was just a way to feel easier about being a gun man.'

'I take it serious,' Cole said. 'Who the hell am I if I don't?'

'What if you had to go against the law someday?' I said.

'Goddamn it, Everett,' Cole said. 'Is this about something, or are you just trying to bore me to death?'

'Just musing,' I said.

'Well, muse about fucking or something,' Cole said.

'Sure,' I said.

CHAPTER 59

Cole had the morning walk-around, and I had the afternoon. It was somewhere in mid-afternoon when I left my horse out front and went into the Boston House. As was usually the case these days, Allie was playing and Bragg was leaning on the piano. If Cole had ever noticed, he hadn't said.

I took the deputy marshal star off my shirt and walked over to the bar with it.

'Willis,' I said to the bartender, 'give this to Virgil Cole next time he's in.'

McDonough looked at the star and at me and started to say something. I took a gun out of my side pocket and placed it on the bar.

'And give this to Bragg when he asks for it,' I said.

'Everett . . .'

'Just do it,' I said and turned away.

I walked across the room to the piano and said, 'Bragg.' He turned and I hit him in the face and knocked him down. The room got quiet. Allie sucked in some air and stared at me with her eyes wide. But she didn't say anything, and there was excitement in her face. On the floor, Bragg was trying to collect himself.

'What the hell are you doing?' he said.

'You are a lying, back-shooting, cowardly sonova bitch,' I said loud, so the whole room would hear me.

Bragg was scrambling to his feet.

'What is this, what is this?' he said.

'I'll be out in the street,' I said. 'You heeled?'

'I don't have a gun,' Bragg said.

'Will has got one for you. I'll be outside.'

'You can't. Christ, you're a deputy marshal. You can't just call me out.'

I slapped him in the face.

'I'm going outside,' I said. 'If you don't come out with a gun, I'll come back in and kill you here.'

Most men can't take a slap in the face. Especially in front of people they want to impress. Especially when they've convinced themselves that they are the herd bull in town.

'You sonova bitch,' Bragg said. 'You think you can pull on me without Cole to back you up. Get on out in the street, you bastard. I'll be out.'

I turned and walked on out into the street. I took the gun out of my holster and held it at my side. Then I waited. To my left, I heard Cole's voice.

'Everett,' he said.

I kept watching the saloon.

'Katie Goode run down and told me,' Cole said.

'Leave it be, Virgil,' I said.

Bragg came out of the saloon and looked uneasily at Cole.

'Cole's not in this,' I said to Bragg.

'Just hold it,' Cole said. 'What's this about, Everett.'

'I ever ask you for anything, Virgil?'

'No.'

'This one time, leave it alone. It's just Bragg and me.'

'Everett, I can't . . .'

'This once, Virgil. This one favor.'

Cole was silent. Bragg stood on the boardwalk of the Boston House. He was all in black with a high, black hat. He carried the gun I'd left for him down by his side. It was so still, I could hear Cole breathing for a moment.

'Okay,' Cole said.

The silence got tighter. I looked at Bragg. It's a trick that Cole had taught me. Look at the whole person, not his eyes, or his shoulder or his gun hand, all of him, so you can react to any movement. I waited. Nothing stirred. If there had been a breeze, it had died. I waited. I knew Bragg would break. And he did. In the slow, almost lyrical way catastrophe happens, he raised his gun hand, and I shot him in the middle, and he fell slowly, beginning to double over at the impact, trying to get off a shot and falling facedown, dead on the boardwalk in front of the saloon. I opened the cylinder, ejected the empty shell, put in a fresh round, snapped the cylinder shut, and put my gun back in the holster. Then I went and hugged Cole, got on my horse, and rode past the marshal's office and on out of town.

In the hills beyond Bragg's ranch, I saw the appaloosa, nervously herding his mares along toward fresh pasture. *He's got the mares* I thought. *But the mare's got him, too.*

Then I turned my horse straight into the afternoon sun and rode west at an easy pace. It was going to be a long ride, and there was no reason to hurry.